On the Edge

Jamie Hill

Published by Jamie Hill, 2022.

This is a work of fiction. Similarities to real people, places, or events are entirely coincidental, although Kansas City is indeed real.

ON THE EDGE

Third edition. July 16, 2022

Copyright © 2022 Jamie Hill

Written by Jamie Hill

Cover Art by Michelle Lee

To Tim, with love

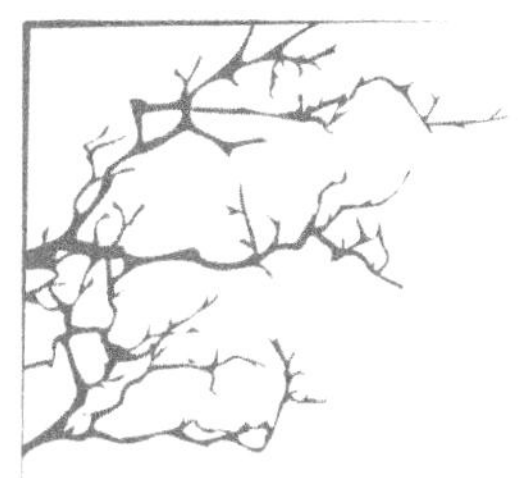

Chapter One

"I THINK MY HOUSE IS haunted. Either that, or I'm losing my mind." The petite woman spoke matter-of-factly, a serious expression on her face.

Jake Gilford looked her over carefully, gauging his first impression. She was pretty, her caramel-colored skin slightly darker than his summer tan. Black-as-coal hair in springy ringlets touched her shoulders. Her eyes were a shade lighter, chocolate-colored, and definitely piercing as they gazed at him directly. She was a small woman, but shapely. He couldn't help but notice the way her hips filled out a tight pair of faded jeans. *Which doesn't mean she's not a nutcase.* He smiled politely. "Miss Wheeler?"

"Of course I'm Jocelyn Wheeler," she snapped, stepping back so he could come inside. "I phoned Chief Taylor about my situation. He assured me he'd send his best detective. I assume that'd be you, Detective...?" She shot him a look, which indicated her skepticism.

He forced another smile, and brushed past her, entering the old house. "Gilford. Jake Gilford. The Chief told me this was a special case. Something about him and your father being old friends—"

"They were. My father died a few months ago, and I'm here to settle his estate—the largest part of which is this house."

He took in as much as he could of the huge, ornately furnished house. If she stood to inherit everything, she'd become a rich woman. He glanced at her—she fidgeted as she looked around, warily. *A rich, nutty woman.* "I'm sorry for your loss."

She shrugged, crossed her arms and rubbed them, as if warding off a chill. "We weren't close."

"Which explains why your father died a few months ago, and you're just now showing up." He ran a finger over the porcelain statue of a zebra, which sat on a side table. There was a lot of wild animal paraphernalia. He wondered about the former occupant of the house. *Big game hunter-type?*

"Actually, I didn't know he was my father until recently. He wrote me before his death."

Jake arched his eyebrow, surprised. "You never knew him?"

"Nope. It was just Mama and me all those years. She told me bits and pieces when I asked, but never mentioned his name. We were happy, and I never asked too many questions. Imagine my surprise to get his letter."

"Yeah." He scratched his stubbled chin. Now he wished he hadn't been running late that morning, or had least taken time to shave. He often sported a three-day beard growth, and liked the way it made him look. But, judging by the way she gazed at him, he wondered if it made him look lazy to this beautiful woman who had a hint of a Southern twang in her voice. "Did he offer any explanation about why he stayed away?"

"Oh, sure." She dropped into a large, overstuffed, brown leather chair, which dwarfed her small frame. "He said Mama understood, they both thought it was the right thing to do at the time. He'd been traveling through the south when they met, and had their thing. They kept in touch for a while, but when she found out she was pregnant—well, it was a problem. White man, black woman...you know. Some people still had prejudices back then." She snorted. "Some people still have prejudices now."

He had to chuckle at that. "No doubt. But in my opinion, it's one of the stupidest excuses I've ever heard. It's hard to believe your father had trouble accepting a half-black daughter. He apparently didn't have a problem sleeping with your mother."

"People can be stupid."

"As a cop, I understand that all too well. But I still find it strange."

She cocked her head, and stared at him. "Why's it so hard to believe?"

Jake shifted uncomfortably from one foot to the other, finally decided to be honest. "Frankly, you're not too tough to look at, Miss Wheeler." Her eyes widened, and he felt his face flush, but he continued, "I mean, you were probably a pretty cute baby. It was his loss, not seeing you grow up. Any man should be proud to have a daughter like you."

She rose from the chair, and had to look up, nearly a foot, to meet his gaze. "I guess twenty-four years ago he didn't think so. There was something about it being delicate in his line of work, but who knows? That might have been just a load of bull. Whatever the case, it seems when he found out he was dying, he wanted to make contact with me. Mama wasn't thrilled, especially when I told her I wanted to come here and stay in his house for a while. It took a long time to convince her, and I didn't make it before he passed away." She turned from him. "I would have liked to have met him, but in some ways, this is easier."

Her shoulders trembled. For an instant, Jake wanted to reach out and comfort her. Political correctness got the best of him and hanging back, he chose his next words carefully. "There's something strange going on in the house, here?"

With a quick swipe of her forearm over her eyes, she turned back to him. "Oh, yeah. It's more than all the creepy animal statues, too. I hear noises in the night. Not just animals, though there's plenty of growling. I've heard trains, boat horns—all kinds of loud, out of place, sounds."

"I can see why you'd be on edge." He hoped his tone was soothing, placating.

"I'm not *on edge*, Detective Gilford. I'm scared shitless."

He choked back a laugh at her frankness, realizing she didn't want to be babied. She seemed sincere, so maybe there was something to what she said. In any case, he was given the job of finding out. "I understand. Why don't you show me around the house and we'll go from there."

"What are you looking for?" Suspicion shone in her eyes.

Hoping to quell it, he smiled again. "I'll let you know when I find it."

The corners of her mouth turned upward, but she still appeared nervous and wary as she moved about the house. Jake watched her for the first few minutes of the tour. He imagined she had a beautiful smile, wondered what he'd have to do to see it.

When he discovered they were in the kitchen, and couldn't remember how they got there, he decided he'd better focus on the house. Hopefully, there'd be time to focus on the stunning Miss Wheeler later.

The huge dwelling had two stories above the main floor, and what appeared, at first glance, to be a dark, musty cellar. He saved that for last, figuring whatever he was looking for was very possibly hidden down there.

Room by room Jake checked closets, cabinets, and every little hidey-hole he could find. Jocelyn followed, not saying much, but close by. By the time he'd poked and prodded through the last bedroom on the highest floor, she asked again, "What are you looking for?"

"I'm not exactly sure. I just wanted to get the feel of the place."

"I've looked for tape players, and other electronic devices, that might make the sounds I've been hearing. There aren't any."

He shrugged. "This is a big place. Electronics are getting smaller and smaller, you may have overlooked whatever it is."

"I may have. Or this stinking place is haunted. That's the direction I'm leaning after almost two weeks here."

"I don't believe in ghosts." They returned to the kitchen. "I believe in facts, and hard evidence. If I nose around enough, I'm sure I'll come up with something."

She pulled open the refrigerator door, and took out a glass pitcher. "I hope so. I can't take too many more sleepless nights. It's making me punchy and cranky. I'm sorry; I'm usually not this way. Can I offer you some tea?"

"Sure." He leaned against the counter, and watched her pull two glasses from the cabinet. While she added ice, a thought occurred to him. "You mentioned you're from the south?"

She nodded. "Alabama, originally. Mama and I moved to New Orleans after Hurricane Katrina."

"Moved there after the hurricane?" he asked, surprised. Most people had moved away then.

"Mama's a nurse. She had friends there and wanted to help rebuild. There's still so much to be done, even now." Raising the pitcher to pour, she hesitated when he touched her arm.

"The reason I asked is...most people from the south drink sweet tea. Is that what this is?"

"Of course."

"I'll take a pass, if you don't mind. I was born and raised right here in Kansas City. The only thing I want sweet is my barbecue sauce."

Without skipping a beat, she poured tea in one glass and filled the other with water from the tap. "Here you go, Detective. I'm afraid I'm addicted to this stuff, so it's all I have to offer you besides water."

He accepted the drink. "Water is perfect, thanks. Please, call me Jake."

"My friends call me Joss." She raised her glass in a toast, and they eyed each other as they drank.

"Joss," he repeated. "I like that." Jake continued watching her, and thought, briefly, that he liked *her*. She wasn't in the best situation, but he could tell she had a sense of humor and a feisty attitude. She was certainly beautiful. He hadn't exaggerated when he'd said she was easy on the eyes. It wouldn't take much for him to forget why he was there, but that wouldn't be right. She needed help, and he was determined to provide it.

Her appealing scent was distracting. Jake smelled gardenias, and something earthy he couldn't identify. It took all the control he could muster to step away, finish his water, and set the glass down. "I should check the cellar."

She reached for a flashlight, and handed it to him. "You'll want this. There's a pull-chain light in the center of the room, but that's it."

"Thanks. Coming with me?"

"Not a chance. Last time I was down there, I saw something that looked like a lizard slither by. That was it for me."

Laughing, he opened the cellar door. "Ah, come on! You have lizards down south. I hear they're quite prevalent in Alabama, probably Louisiana too."

"Not where I live." She shuddered and waved him on. "I'll be right here when you get back."

"Yes ma'am." Still chuckling, he made his way down the steep, wooden steps. It wasn't the nicest basement he'd ever been in, but not the worst, either. When he was a uniformed cop on the beat, he had the fortune—or misfortune—of helping apprehend a serial killer who'd kept body parts, in barrels, in his basement. The nutcase used bleach to clean up. To this day, Jake couldn't smell chlorine without remembering the stinking, rotten stench he and his partner had stumbled into. That was the worst basement he'd ever been in.

This one was dank and musty but once he yanked the chain and the light came on it looked fairly non-threatening. He checked the obvious places, finding little more than a mouse, and a few spiders. He'd keep that information to himself, and bring a few traps the next time he came around. Joss appeared shaken enough; he wasn't sure how she'd handle a mouse problem.

"That wasn't so bad," he announced, when she met him at the top of the steps.

"Any lizards?"

"Not even a little one, I promise." He dusted off his shirtsleeves and went to the sink, where he refilled his water glass.

"So you think I'm crazy." She seemed sad.

I hate that. "Of course I don't. I haven't heard anything, so I can't say what's going on. But I believe that something's not right."

"That's putting it mildly." Joss crossed her arms, and sighed.

Jake took another drink, then lowered his glass. "The noises only happen at night?"

"Yes."

He inhaled, and let his breath out slowly. "I suppose I could set up a stake-out, get the chief to assign a couple of men—"

"Could you stay?" She moved closer to him. "I sort of trust you, after spending the last few hours with you. I'd rather not have to get to know any more cops."

"You, sort of, trust me," he repeated, with a sly grin. "Sounds like high praise coming from a jittery woman."

Her cheeks flushed pink. "I'm not jittery. I'm scared as hell, remember. I feel like I'm losing my mind. I've got to figure out what's going on here and I can't do it by myself."

"I'm going to help you," he said quickly. He realized, at that moment, that he had no intention of turning her over to other officers. This was his case, and he wanted her to be his responsibility. "I'll stay tonight, if you're sure that's what you want."

"I absolutely do." She seemed relieved. "I can make you a bed in one of the guestrooms."

"That won't be necessary. Just a pot of coffee, if you have any. I'll camp out on the sofa, and do a bit of wandering throughout the night."

"I have coffee." She nodded. "I don't have much to eat. I need to go to the store, but I haven't had the energy the last few days."

"Do you like Chinese food?"

"Sure."

"I'm going to run to the office, tie up a few loose ends, then stop by my place for a couple of things. I can pick up dinner on my way back, if you like."

"That sounds perfect. You'll be back before dark?"

"For sure. Six-thirty at the latest. You'll be okay until I get back?"

Joss nodded and rubbed her arms again. "Thank you, Jake. I feel better already."

He stopped at the front door. "Any special requests from our local Chinese joint, Wong Foo's?"

"I like Moo Shu."

"Pork or chicken?"

"Surprise me." She finally smiled. Her face lit up in a brilliant, twinkling glow.

It was as beautiful as he'd expected, and he grinned in return. With a quick wink, he squeezed her arm gently, and slipped out the door.

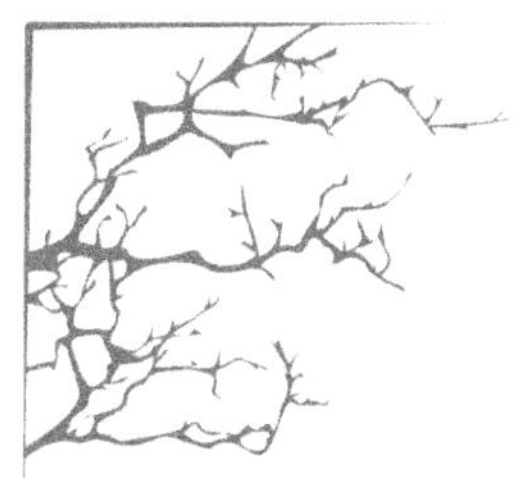

Chapter Two

WHEN HE RETURNED WITH the food, he saw she'd set out plates, napkins and silverware on the coffee table in front of the sofa.

"I thought this would be more comfortable than the kitchen." She ushered him to the sofa, and took a seat on one end. "Do you mind?"

"Not a bit. I'm all about comfort." He kicked his shoes off and settled in, as she piled food on his plate. They made small talk while they ate—discussed books, movies, along with various likes and dislikes.

After dinner, Jake drank coffee. It'd been a while since he'd been on a stake-out, and usually he had his partner to talk to. Being alone would make it much more difficult to stay awake. Hopefully, the coffee would help.

Joss finished her tea and they cleaned up the dinner dishes together. "Are you sure you don't want me to show you a guestroom?"

"Nah, thanks. I'm going to try not to sleep. Just go to bed. Lock yourself in. You might hear me wandering around. Call out if you're concerned, I'll let you know where I am. Hopefully, I can find the source of the noise."

She pulled a blanket and pillow from a linen closet, and set them on the sofa. "You should try to sleep. You'll hear it when it starts; don't worry about sleeping through it."

He smiled. "I just want to stay alert."

She covered her mouth as she yawned, then she stretched. "No chance of that here. I'm beat."

"Try to relax. I intend to figure this thing out."

Joss nodded. "I'll try. Thanks, Jake. Goodnight."

"Goodnight." He watched her climb the stairs to her room on the second floor. Every step appeared to be an effort. *She must really be exhausted.* With any luck, he'd put an end to her worries soon.

He grabbed his overnight bag, pulled a few things out and headed to the first floor bathroom. Jake brushed his teeth then splashed water on his face. Rubbing his eyes, he looked at himself in the mirror. Shaggy brown hair curled over his ears and around his collar, begging for a trim. He worked long hours and rarely thought about his appearance. When he did think about it, barber shops were closed. The high priced clip joints in the mall were probably open, but he didn't worry enough about his hair to spend big bucks on it.

He *had* taken time to shave when he ran home earlier. After meeting Joss, he was suddenly thinking about the things he usually didn't bother with. Something about her interested him, and he wanted to get to know her better. She seemed dejected, which made him want to help her all the more.

When darkness fell he went on high alert, prepared for action if the strange noises started. The house was quiet as he slipped from room to room, looking for anything unusual. He didn't see, or hear, anything out of the ordinary.

The coffeepot was empty. Jake debated making more, when the grandfather clock in the hall struck two a.m. He didn't really want more coffee, just needed to close his eyes for a minute. The house was locked tight, he knew that. There was nothing more he could do, unless something happened. He was doubtful anything would. As he settled against the pillow on the sofa, he wondered what he'd say to Joss in the morning if it was a quiet night. She'd probably be pissed that nothing happened while he was there, instead of being grateful for a good night's sleep. As much as he loved women, he knew that's how they thought. Chuckling, he closed his eyes.

The clock chimed four a.m. Jake stretched on the sofa. He hated clocks that sounded on the hour. Most people slept through the noise, but he never could. Just as the fourth knell sounded, he closed his eyes in search of more sleep.

Blaring sirens pealed through the house, followed by the roar of racing engines. Jake sprang from the sofa, fully awake, and ran for the stairs. The wails and revving sounds became almost unbearable as he reached the second floor. He covered his ears. *Which room are they coming from? And how could they be so blasted loud?*

He threw open the door to the first bedroom but before he could go in Joss appeared in the hall. Her hands covered her ears, tears streaked her face. "Make it stop!"

Torn between tracking the sounds and comforting her, his heart got the better of him. He reached for her, pulled her into his arms. "Shhhh. It'll be okay." He nestled her face into his chest, so one of her ears was pressed against him. He covered the other with his hand. Bending to press his lips to the top of her head, he continued soothing her, hoping his voice was loud enough to be heard above the din. "Nothing's going to hurt you. I'm here. I've got you."

Joss clung to him, her tiny body shaking. He wrapped his other arm tightly around her, and rocked back and forth. "It'll stop soon." When he realized he didn't know how long the noises had lasted in the past, he added, "I hope."

He heard her snicker, and thought it was a good sign. Maybe more humor was called for. "Ever wanted to be the flag waver at the Daytona 500?"

"No!" she yelled, as the house fell silent. "Oh! Sorry."

Jake grinned, and turned her loose. "No problem. I won't be able to hear for a while, anyway. Stay here. I need to look around."

"Don't leave me!"

He squeezed her shoulders. "I'll be right back. Hang tight." Jogging down the stairs, he checked all the doors, windows, even went into the cellar, but all was normal. Back upstairs, he went into each room searching for something—anything—unusual.

Joss was sitting on the edge of her bed when he returned. "Anything?"

"No, damn it," he muttered. "I need to keep looking around while the noise is blasting. Maybe next time I can track its source."

She looked up at him. "Next time?"

"Of course."

Standing, she continued to look into his eyes. "That'll be tomorrow. It never happens twice in one night."

He nodded. "Tomorrow night, then. I promised to help you out, and I meant it."

"You're a good cop. But maybe what I need is a ghost buster."

"I don't think so, Joss." He took a step toward her. "I told you, I don't believe in ghosts. There's something fishy going on here. I'm pretty sure what you need is a cop."

She touched the lapel of his button-down shirt. "I could use a friend, I know that much."

He gazed at the beauty before him. She wore nothing but a short, soft cotton nightgown, which was tantalizingly sheer. "Joss," he began, then hesitated. This was a bad idea. "I, uh, need to go downstairs."

She grabbed the front of his shirt and pulled him closer. "I wish you'd stay. I really don't want to be alone."

He nodded to a chair in the corner. "I'll sit over there until you fall asleep, if that'll help."

"Jake," she murmured. Her eyes were half-closed, unfocused, and she appeared groggy. "Kiss me."

He moved her toward the bed. "I'm sure I'd enjoy that. But it's not going to happen when you're only half awake, and I'm on duty. Get some sleep, we'll talk in the morning."

"But—"

"Sleep." He cut the protest off, settled her in bed, and drew the covers up over her. "I'll see you tomorrow."

She sighed, snuggled in, and seemed to fall asleep instantly. He stood by the door watching her for a few minutes, then returned to the main floor. It was doubtful he'd get any more sleep, but he had to try. He'd need all his energy and his wits about him to figure this craziness out. But he'd figure it out. *I have to.*

JAKE STARED AT THE living room ceiling. The grandfather clock, which didn't seem so noisy anymore, chimed nine a.m. He knew he should get up, but wasn't quite ready. He did some of his best thinking in the morning hours, when things were fresh.

Joss hadn't imagined the noise. It was as real as he was. There had to be a logical explanation for where it came from. Why was a different matter, and probably not so easily explained.

He'd work on one thing at a time. First, the where. They might have to tear the house apart to find the source. He'd start on that first thing. No, second thing, after a shower. He needed a morning shower to clear his head. *And breakfast.* He was hungry—could definitely eat. Tearing the house apart would be the third thing on his list of things to do, after a shower and breakfast. Jake smiled to himself, wondering if everyone divided their life into neat little lists like he did, or if he was a total nut. A game plan in mind, he tossed his legs over the side of the sofa and sat up.

Glancing around the room, he had a sudden thought. *If I am a nut, I fit right into this house.* The head of a buck stared at him from above the fireplace. A stuffed bobcat stood on the bricks next to the hearth. Several other animals were placed strategically around the room. He wasn't sure if they'd all been alive at some point, or if they were imitations, but he was sure they were flat out creepy. He liked animals as much as the next guy, but this was ridiculous.

Making his way to the shower, Jake let the water run a minute before he stripped, and stepped in. He held his face under the nozzle while water flooded over him. It was hot and steamy, which did nothing to help his thoughts of Joss.

But thinking of her in that way didn't feel right. He wanted more than her being his pin-up girl. He suspected she wanted more from him, as well. If he could solve her case, he knew he wanted to explore further possibilities with Joss. For now, he needed to focus. He turned the nozzle to cold, and quickly finished his shower.

Jake dressed in a fresh set of jeans and a t-shirt, with a button down shirt over the top. He towel-dried his unruly hair, straightened the bathroom when he was done, and shoved everything back into his bag. When he stepped out, Joss was at the foot of the stairs.

"Good morning." She looked perky and bright, in a red blouse over jeans.

"Good morning. You look refreshed. How'd you sleep?"

"After the races ended, I slept pretty well. I had some weird dreams, though. One of them involved my putting the moves on you, and I know that would never have happened in real life." She grinned at him.

He laughed. "A proper Southern woman such as yourself? No way. It was all a dream."

She stood next to him, and nudged his elbow with hers. "I'm really sorry about that. Those noises make me crazy—I go a little nuts. Sometimes I don't feel like myself at all."

"So you're saying a woman would have to be crazy to put the moves on me?"

"No!" she replied quickly, then glanced up and realized he was teasing. "You smart ass!"

"Better than being a dumb ass, I always say." He followed her into the kitchen.

She opened the refrigerator, and peered inside. "I have eggs and some cheese. I could make an omelet for breakfast."

"That sounds great. I was going to say I could eat a horse, but there might be a stuffed one around here somewhere."

"No kidding. Isn't it bizarre?" She got food, along with the pitcher of tea, from the fridge. "If I was going to live here, I'd have to get rid of the menagerie right away." Reaching for a glass in the cabinet, she poured some tea and sipped it. "Can I fix you some coffee?"

"Half a pot, maybe. I'll make it, if you're fixing eggs."

"Help yourself." She motioned to the counter, then turned to the stove.

Jake picked up the tea pitcher, and sniffed. "Starting pretty early on this stuff."

She laughed. "There's no vodka in it, I promise. Just Mama's sweet tea recipe. You should try it."

He feigned a shiver. "No thanks." After reaching for the coffee filters in the cabinet where Joss had gotten them the previous night, he made some coffee, then leaned against the counter while she cooked. "So, you haven't decided about living here? Once your problem is solved, that is."

"My problem," she repeated. "You make it sound so clinical. I'm still not convinced the place isn't haunted. And no, I don't care to live in a freaking haunted house. Even if you prove to me it's not, I don't know that I could stay here. Every day that goes by makes me dislike the place a little more."

He cocked his head as he listened. "Why stay? There's nothing holding you here. Tell the lawyer to sell the place and send your check to New Orleans."

She flipped the eggs and faced him, appearing thoughtful. "I considered that. Believe me, after that first night, I was packed and ready to take off. But something niggled at me—a little feeling in the pit of my stomach, that asked, 'Why are you letting them chase you out?' The more I thought about it, the more sense it made. This is my house now. I should be able to stay here if I want."

He nodded. "That's true. But, you told me several times this place scares the heck out of you. I'd think you'd want to catch the next train for The Big Easy."

She smiled, and served omelets on two plates. They grabbed drinks and utensils, then sat at the table. "If you must know, things in The Big Easy aren't so easy these days. Mama and I went round and round about the whole Edward Cooper issue. She's still mad that I came here."

Jake took a bite of his omelet, and paused to savor it. "This is fantastic," he motioned with his fork. "Edward Cooper was your father?"

"Thank you." She smiled. "Yes, he was."

He devoured the omelet, sipped coffee, and continued to mull things over. "So you and your mother argued. That's why you want to stay here? No place else to go?"

"You ask a lot of questions, detective."

"All part of the job." Jake glanced at his watch. "Speaking of which, I'm off duty in an hour. I'd like to comb through the house, one more time, before I have to go get a couple of things done."

Her eyes widened. "You're leaving?"

He reached for her hand, and squeezed. "I'll be back. I don't have any plans this weekend, other than solving the mystery of this house."

"But you won't be on duty?" She looked skeptical.

"It doesn't matter. If I need back up, I can get it. Sunday is technically my day off. No big deal."

"You're willing to spend your day off helping me?"

Jake almost laughed, but caught himself. He bent forward and, in a serious tone, said, "It's a tough duty, but yeah, I'll step up and volunteer."

Joss blushed. She reached for their plates and stood, going to the sink.

"Let me help you." He followed, taking the plates from her.

"We could try out the dishwasher."

"Nah, this'll just take a minute." He washed and she dried, so they were done quickly.

Joss folded her dishtowel and laid it on the counter. "You're pretty handy to have around."

He grinned. "Thanks. I do my best."

She licked her lips as she gazed into his eyes.

They were inches apart. For a moment, he could barely breathe. He'd never seen eyes so brown and clear, lips so perfect, too kissable to ignore. "Joss," he murmured.

"Do you always have to talk?" She stood on tiptoes and reached up, lowering his mouth to hers.

He gave in, and returned the kiss. Her lips tasted as good as they looked.

Jake groaned, and pulled away. "That was better than I'd imagined, and I have a fine imagination."

She grinned, and looked him up and down. "If I had to wager, I'd bet you have lots of fine parts."

He laughed and loosened her hand from his shirt. Kissing her knuckles, he squeezed and swung her hand back and forth between them. "Are you going to help me look around again? Eventually we're going to spot something."

"Why not? I've got nothing but time."

"Then let's go. I'm feeling lucky."

"Ha!" she smirked.

Grinning, he pushed her out of the kitchen.

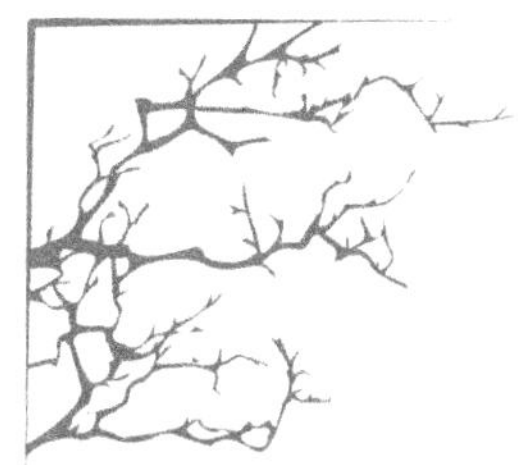

Chapter Three

HIS SECOND TRIP THROUGH the house produced no results, but Jake wasn't discouraged. He knew it was simply a matter of time before he uncovered the where. Then, the real work would begin, tackling the who and perhaps more importantly, the why.

He left Joss going through papers in the study, and went to the police department to take care of his own paperwork. Several hours later he swung by his house and packed a few more clothes. He headed back to Joss's with a carryout pepperoni and mushroom pizza.

"That smells great." She took the box and set it on the kitchen table. "I'm starving!"

"Me too," he agreed. "I haven't eaten since the eggs." He got out plates and napkins. "Everything quiet here?"

"Too quiet," she muttered, and bit into a piece of pizza before sitting down.

He watched her movements, noticed that she seemed agitated again. She'd told him yesterday, the closer it got to nightfall, the more nervous she became. He wondered if that was the only reason. "You okay?"

"Sure. Just hungry." When she glanced at him, he saw her eyes were glassy. *What's going on?*

The food—or his return—seemed to calm her. They talked and joked as they ate, then moved to the sofa.

"You might want to sleep down here tonight," he suggested. "It's not as noisy."

"Where will you be sleeping?" She cozied up next to him.

"Joss." He pulled back.

"Why do you keep doing that? Every time I touch you, you move away. A girl might start to wonder."

He brushed a strand of hair from her face. "I think we need to take things slow. Believe me, that's not what all of me thinks. But I'm trying to keep a clear head."

She ran the back of a finger down the side of his face. "You told me you were off duty."

"I am." He shifted uncomfortably. The closer she got, the harder he found it to resist.

"Then relax," she murmured, leaning in to nuzzle his neck.

Jake groaned, tired of struggling, ready to take her advice. He was off duty, they were both adults—maybe it was time to stop thinking so much. He sunk lower into the sofa, and she rolled on top of him.

Their lips met and they kissed, then she was gone again, nibbling his ear. He dragged his hands up her back, caressing through the soft blouse.

He'd just zeroed in on her neck when something roared, setting off an ear-splitting pandemonium of animal noises. "Son of a—!" He looked around. It had grown dark outside and he hadn't noticed. *I'm noticing now.*

His eyes locked on hers, and he saw a brief flash of terror. "Stay here!" He bolted for the stairs.

The animal noises grew louder as Jake ascended the stairs. In Joss's bedroom and the room next to it, the sound created an ear-drum shattering din. He struggled to keep searching, even as the noise grew intensely painful.

The source was tough to pinpoint, but he estimated it was coming from the ceiling. There was a floor above them. He'd figure out which rooms were above these two and inspect the floorboards closely.

The racket continued, louder than the Kansas City Zoo's monkey house at feeding time. His head pounded. He thought about dashing down the stairs, grabbing Joss, and getting the hell out, even though he knew that wouldn't accomplish anything. He worked through the pain, forcing himself up to the third floor.

It was a few decibels quieter there. Catching his breath, he tried to maintain control. Estimating which room was above Joss's, he grasped the Oriental rug covering the hardwood floor and yanked it back.

The house fell silent. Jake realized his breathing was now the loudest thing in the room. He steadied himself, forced a calmness he didn't really feel, and dropped to the floor. He carefully ran his fingers along the cracks, searching for a raised board.

"It's over," Joss said from the doorway.

He jumped at the sound of her voice, then smiled grimly. "Please don't do that."

"Sorry. Did you find anything?"

"I think I pinpointed where the noise is coming from. It was loudest in your bedroom ceiling, and in the ceiling of the yellow room next to it."

She dropped to her knees next to him. "You think they put something under the floorboards? I never thought to look here."

"Me either," he admitted. "Let's do it now."

Joss ran her hands over the cracks and muttered, "Not exactly what I wanted to be doing."

He agreed. "I hear you. It'll be nice when we figure this out, so we can concentrate on other things."

"Keep looking," she instructed firmly.

He chortled. "Yes, ma'am."

They ran their hands over every inch of the floor, but couldn't find even one nail out of place. After giving the next room the same treatment, and again finding nothing, Jake rose disgustedly, wiping his hands on his jeans. "I thought for sure we'd find a loose floor board."

"It was a good idea." She stood, dusting her hands off as he had. "I'm thirsty. Let's get something to drink."

He followed her down the stairs. "Got any beer?"

"No. I think there's some wine, though. Want me to look?"

"Nah, thanks." He washed his hands in the kitchen sink, and got a glass of water.

Joss poured the last glass of tea from the pitcher. She went to the cabinet and got what looked like a homemade tea bag, then put the kettle on to boil.

"Home brew," he commented, drinking deeply of the cold tap water.

"Yep. Special recipe, I keep telling you."

"How much caffeine is in there?" He lifted the bag and sniffed it. There was an unusual fragrance he couldn't quite place.

"Same as in regular tea. Mama added herbs and dried fruit, then I add the sugar."

"I see." He watched her prepare the tea, and yawned. "Sounds like a lot of work."

"It's worth it." She returned the pitcher to the fridge. Turning to him, she sighed. "You look beat."

Jake yawned again. "It's been a long couple of days."

"Come on." Taking him by the hand, she led him to the living room sofa. "One nice feature about this place. The sofa is roomy." Dragging a couple pillows to one end, she rolled on and patted the space next to her.

"Joss—"

"Shhh! Come on." She patted the sofa again.

He lay next to her, and she snuggled into his chest, tossing a blanket over them both.

"I know you're tired. I am too. For some reason, I think I'll sleep better in your arms."

He smiled, and kissed the top of her head. "Sounds good to me. 'Night, beautiful."

"Goodnight." She patted his chest a few times.

When her breathing slowed and became regular, he knew she'd fallen asleep. Jake drew one hand through her hair. He'd been afraid that being this close would be uncomfortable—that all he'd think about was sex and never get to sleep. Having Joss sprawled next to him, one knee over his, her head on his chest, was, at that moment, the most restful thing he could imagine. He closed his eyes, and smiled.

When he opened his eyes again she was gone. Morning sun shone through the front windows. Jake sat up and rubbed his face. He couldn't believe he'd slept so soundly. He never even heard the chiming of the grandfather clock in the hall. "Joss?"

There was no answer. He looked in the kitchen, then moved to the bottom of the stairs. The sound of running water upstairs confirmed she was there, so he went to clean up.

Even with a good night's rest, he still felt tired. The oppressiveness of the house was sucking the energy from him. He needed to get away, at least for a while. Hopefully he'd convince Joss to go with him. If he felt this way, after just two nights, he couldn't imagine how she felt after two weeks in the creepy mansion.

She appeared cheerful when they met in the kitchen. "Good morning." Joss stood on tiptoes to press a small kiss on his lips. "You were sleeping soundly. I hope I didn't wake you."

"Not at all. I can't believe how well I slept."

She smiled. "Today we have toast. After that I'll be forced to go to the grocery store."

"Toast is fine, and coffee. Must have coffee."

"Help yourself." She motioned to the counter.

He brewed a half-pot while she made toast, and they ate at the kitchen table. "I had another idea," Jake said. "A house this size has to have an attic. Why haven't I noticed the door to one?"

She shrugged. "I've never seen it."

"This morning we're going to search for it. It's got to be here. Then this afternoon, I hoped maybe we could get out. Autumn is beautiful in Kansas. We could take a drive down by the river."

"A drive sounds nice."

"Good." He squeezed her hand, and they finished eating. Setting their plates and the knife in the sink, he said, "I'd like to walk around the exterior of the house."

"Let's go." Joss slipped into her shoes and led him out.

He made mental notes as they looked around. The house was old, but well kept. There wasn't much stuff sitting outside. He thought about everything that collected outside his own house. The curled up garden hose, a bottle of weed killer, muddy boots by the back door—all signs that his home was lived in, cared for. There were no signs of anything here.

There was a round window at the uppermost peak of the house, and he knew he'd never been in a room with a round window. It looked like there was an attic. "Let's go find it," he told Joss, taking her by the hand, and heading back inside.

"I noticed that window, but never gave it a second thought."

"That's how we'll figure this thing out—perseverance, second thoughts, third thoughts—whatever it takes. Now, how do we get into that attic?"

They searched the third floor of the house, inspecting ceilings this time. Finally, in the last bedroom's smallest closet, he found it. An inset tile pushed upward, leading to a black, yawning space. "This is it. We'll need something to stand on, and flashlights."

She pointed to an ottoman. "You can climb on that. I left the flashlights in my room. Be right back."

"Great, thanks." Jake shoved the ottoman under the opening, climbed on it and poked his head in. There was a sliver of light from the round window, but the attic was mostly dark. Something scurried across the floor, and he decided to wait for the flashlight.

"Here you go." She handed up the bigger of the two lights she held. "I'll use this one."

"Are you sure you want to come up? It's dark and smells musty."

Joss snorted. "I might have given you the impression that I'm delicate, but I'm really not. I can handle it."

"Suit yourself." He reached up to set the flashlight on the attic floor. Positioning his hands on either side of the opening above him, he pulled himself up into the dark room.

Picking up his flashlight, he switched it on, just in time to see a mouse disappearing under some old furniture. He blew out a breath. Glancing down at Joss, he said, "You sure about this? It's dirty and there are some little four-legged friends running around."

"Lizards?"

"Nope, one mouse. But where there's one..."

She waved her hand. "Mice are nothing. Scaly things that shed their skin bother me."

"Okay then. Pull yourself up."

She made a face at him. "I said I wasn't delicate. I never said I was a weightlifter. Could I have a hand, please?"

Jake bent down, grinning. "Not much weight to lift, you little thing."

She grabbed his arm and he pulled her up. When she was standing, facing him in the attic, she told him, "I have plenty of weight. You're just really strong."

Looking her up and down, he couldn't resist adding, "You're weighted in all the right places, I'll grant you that."

Joss laughed. "Sweet talker. Honestly, I'd love to hear more, but maybe later, down by the river or wherever?"

"You got it." He rubbed his thumb over a smudge on her cheek. "Let's see what we can find up here."

She shone her light in the corner. "A bunch of dirty junk."

His knee bumped into a stack of boxes, raising a cloud of dust. "Ugh!"

Joss sneezed.

"Sorry." He moved slower, trying to avoid stirring up more of the gray, smoky dust.

"Not your fault. There's about an inch of dirt on top of everything."

"At least." Opening a box, he found it full of books. It was too dark to make out titles. "We'll either have to bring up more light, or carry this stuff down to go through it. It'd be almost impossible with flashlights."

"I've barely started on the den. This could take forever."

He blazed a trail forward, toeing boxes and trying to get an idea of what was there. "If I were you, I'd hire some nice young men to empty the attic for you. Take the stuff downstairs, clean it off, the whole bit."

"What a great idea. Can we go now, since we have a plan?"

He rolled his eyes. "One more minute. Let's look for a tape player or whatever's making the noise. It didn't sound like it was coming from up here, and we'd likely see prints in all this dust, but we should double check."

"Right behind you." She touched his waist, and they moved deeper into the attic.

"Lots of boxes, some old furniture. Might be some antiques."

"Mama loves antiques," Joss commented. She shone her light on a shape sitting under the window. "What's that?"

Aiming his light alongside hers, he made out the form of a woman in a wooden rocking chair. He took another step forward, Joss clinging to his belt loop, and froze. "What in the world?"

It wasn't a woman, but a skeleton in a woman's dress, wearing a wig and a hat.

Joss screamed, turned and ran.

"Wait!" He spun around, just in time to see her disappear.

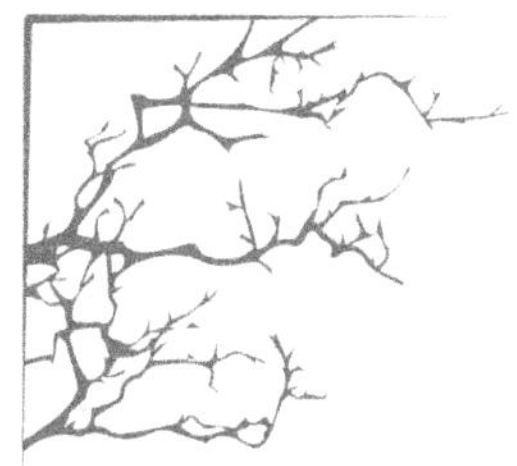

Chapter Four

"JOSS!" HE HEADED BACK toward the opening in the floor.

"I'm over here," she replied, closer than he expected.

"Keep talking. Where?"

"Right here. I fell on a mattress, I think."

Shining his light on her face, he was relieved to see she hadn't fallen out of the attic. "Are you hurt?"

"Just my pride. Can you help me up?"

Jake smiled, offered his hand. "Of course."

She latched on and rose to meet him. "Damn it."

He cupped her face. "You sure you're okay?"

"Yeah."

He pulled her to his chest, hugging her. "I thought you fell through the opening. You could have broken your neck."

"Nothing so dramatic."

He kissed her forehead and released her. "Thank God." They looked at each other for a moment. Moving back to the skeleton, he reached out to touch it. Someone had placed it here, recently. *But why?* "This skeleton is plastic. And clean, very clean. Hardly dusty at all."

"Plastic? But who would put it up here? And what for?"

"All part of the plan to scare you out, I'd say. I hope this convinces you, the house isn't haunted, merely meant to look that way."

"It does." She nodded. "Ghosts are one thing, way out of my control. But now I know this is someone messing with me, and that pisses me off."

"Me too. Let's get out of here, we need some fresh air." He moved to the opening in the floor and clicked off his flashlight. Sitting on the edge, he dropped carefully to the ottoman and steadied himself. Glancing up, he said, "Slowly, now."

Joss followed his lead, sitting before dropping into his arms.

He caught her, held her tight for a moment, then released. They stepped to the floor and faced each other. He raised his flashlight. "Let's put these where we can find them again."

"On my dresser." She led him downstairs.

Joss set both flashlights down and looked in her bureau mirror. "I'm filthy."

He chuckled, pushing back a strand of her hair. "You look good to me."

"Then you're the crazy one. I'm going to wash up before we leave."

"I could probably stand a little of the same. Meet you downstairs."

"Thanks, Jake." She smiled at him.

His heart leapt. *She's pretty, dust-covered or not.* He smiled back and went to the first floor bathroom, where he glanced in the mirror. He was as dirty as she was. The attic was obviously not a high-traffic area. But someone had been up there recently, and he wondered if it was simply scare tactics, or if there was another motive.

He changed his shirt and washed up, then met Joss in the kitchen where she was drinking tea.

"Get you anything?" She held out her glass.

"Yes. A cold beer. I want one now more than ever. Maybe some crab legs to go with it. What do you say?"

Nodding, she set her glass on the counter and reached for her purse. His cell phone rang, and they looked at each other. "I say, answer your phone."

"Novel idea, thanks." He flipped the phone open and punched the talk button. "Gilford!"

"This is Taylor. You were working up a report on the Newsome case, and I need it."

"Oh, right," he muttered to his boss. He'd forgotten about that case when he was assigned this one. "Actually, I'm with Joss Wheeler, and we're working on her problem." He raised his eyebrows, and she covered her mouth with one hand to quiet her laugh.

"I've got to be in court first thing tomorrow morning. I need that report now. Can the Wheeler girl wait?"

Jake stifled a groan. "Sure, boss. I'll be right there."

"By 'right here' do you mean now, or in an hour, Gilford? Just so I know. My kids are waiting for me at home."

"I'm on my way, Sir."

"Thank you." He hung up, and Jake poked his phone off.

"Don't tell me." She looked at him.

He gave her his best puppy dog eyes. "I have to go into the office for a little bit. It won't take long, I promise. I'm really sorry."

"Can I go with you?"

"You'd do that?" He was surprised.

"Sure. I'm ready for a break from this place. I was just getting my mind wrapped around crab legs and beer."

He grinned. "Okay! Let's go."

On the drive to the department, he asked, "Have you seen your father's will?"

"I haven't seen it, exactly. His lawyer told me what was in it."

"Who's the lawyer?"

"His name is Roland Watkins. He gave me the keys to the house."

"But not a copy of the will." It was more a statement than a question.

"I didn't think. I should have asked for one."

"We'll call him tomorrow, and arrange to get one right away."

She looked at him. "You think it matters?"

Jake nodded. "Someone was going to inherit your father's estate before you showed up. I'd like to know who it was."

"I never thought about that."

He hadn't thought of much else, but hadn't voiced the speculation. "We can't do much about it on Sunday. We'll call Watkins tomorrow."

"Sure," she agreed, and glanced at the big building next to where he parked.

He led her in, showing her up to his office. "Have a seat." The waiting area had several chairs, a coffeepot and magazines. "I'll hurry."

"Take your time." She sat and looked around.

He rummaged through his desk for the chief's report. It was nearly done. He added a few details, and handed it over to his supervisor.

"Thanks, Gilford. Sorry to drag you in on your day off."

He shrugged. "It happens."

"So what's the story on Edward Cooper's house? Is his daughter as nutty as she sounded the other day?"

"I don't think so." He nodded toward the waiting room, where Joss leafed through a magazine. "She's terrified, but something strange is going on."

Taylor raised his eyebrows at her. "She said the house is haunted."

"Yeah, I know. I finally got her talked out of that. Someone's behind the spooky happenings she's experienced, I'm sure of it. First thing tomorrow, I'm going to speak with Cooper's lawyer. Someone must have been set to inherit everything before Joss showed up. That's the person I suspect."

The chief nodded. "Sounds reasonable. If you need back up, let me know. Edward was a good man. I was surprised to learn he had a daughter. He never told me about her, but his lawyer verified it. Now I see why he kept it a secret."

"You didn't know her mother was black?"

"No. But that explains a few things. I couldn't figure out why he never mentioned the girl."

Jake scratched his chin. "If race was such an issue with him, why would he sleep with her mother to begin with?"

"Well now," the chief said with a raucous laugh, "Why does any man sleep with a particular woman? Shall we count the reasons?"

"Not necessary." He tried to change the subject. "So, do you know the lawyer?"

"Watkins? Sure, we've met a few times."

"What's your take on the guy?"

He shrugged. "Seems decent, for a lawyer. I've never dealt with him, but never heard of any problems, either."

"Okay, just wondering." Jake moved back toward his desk. "I'm going to take off."

"Me too," Taylor followed him, glancing out to the reception area. "Sorry you have to hold her hand this weekend. Hope you get things settled soon."

"No problem." He pretended to straighten his desk so the boss would leave ahead of him. He didn't feel like making introductions, and couldn't take any more apologies for being forced to spend time with Joss. There was no place he'd rather be.

A couple of minutes after Taylor left, Jake went to the front of the office. "I'm ready. Thanks for being so patient."

She deposited the magazine on a table and stood. "No problem. Was that Chief Taylor?"

"Yes."

"He was in a hurry."

Jake smiled. "He doesn't like working Sundays, either. He's got two small children."

"Really? I thought he was my father's age."

"I think he is. He also has a couple grown children from an earlier marriage."

She nodded, and they headed out. "What about you, Jake? Never wanted to go the wife and family route?"

He grimaced. "That's a loaded question. Let's just say, I may have wanted to, but circumstances always seemed to get in the way." He opened the car door for her, and she got in.

He entered his side and she continued, "Was that a yes or a no? Do you want children?"

"'Course I do, eventually." Starting the engine, he drove to a restaurant he liked, for an early dinner.

"When the circumstances are right?"

He couldn't help but smile again, and glanced over at her. "I guess so. What about you? Are there little ones in your future?"

"Eventually. I'd like to do a few more things with my life, first. Mama wanted me to become a nurse, like her, but I could never get past the emptying bedpans part."

He parked at the Seafood Shack, and turned to her. "I'd imagine it's a lot more rewarding than that."

"Sure it is, but it's not very glamorous. I'm not one to shy away from work, but personally, it's just not my thing."

"Fair enough." He escorted her into the restaurant, where a young, gum-snapping waitress seated them. They ordered crab legs and beer, and he continued talking. "What would you like to do with your life?"

"I don't know. I've had lots of jobs, but nothing that ever truly excited me."

The waitress brought their beers, and Jake raised his glass in a toast. "Here's to discovering what excites you."

She snickered. "I'll drink to that!"

He grinned over the rim of his glass, and they drank. Their food arrived, and they ate while continuing to chat.

After dinner, they walked down to the bank of the river. The temperature was mild, with the hint of a crisp autumn nip in the air. The late afternoon sun caused reflections from nearby businesses to glisten off the water in bright, twinkling spots.

"It's so pretty here," she said, in a dreamy tone.

He slipped an arm around her waist. "You're the pretty one. You look even better out here in the fresh air, away from the house."

"I feel good. I wish we didn't have to go back."

He held her by the waist, turning her to face him. "We don't have to, tonight. We could go to my place and forget about things for a while."

"I'd like that." She curled one hand around the edge of his shirt and raised her face.

He bent, lowering his mouth to hers. Their kiss was slow, lingering, and Jake hated to pull away. The idea of taking her back to his place was exciting. He was ready to go. "Mmm, you taste like crab and beer. Two of my favorite things."

She smiled, still clutching his shirt. "Wonder if there's room for movement on that 'favorite things' list?"

"Oh yeah," he replied, leaning in for another kiss. "I feel things shifting already."

With reluctance, Jake let go of Joss long enough to drive back to his house. It was a short distance, but by the time they got there, he was ready to burst. The evening ahead held great promise.

Joss glanced around as he led her to his front porch. "This is nice."

"Nowhere near as big as your place."

"Not as scary, either."

He couldn't argue with that. He unlocked the door to his ranch-style home, and they stepped in.

"Oh Jake! I love the way you've decorated."

It was a modest bachelor's dwelling, but he'd furnished it in a Southwestern motif with careful attention to detail. The shades of blue and brown were his favorite, and he was pleased that she seemed to like it. He thought it looked good, and he felt comfortable there. "Thanks. I like it."

"You know what I like? Not one wild animal in sight."

He tossed his keys on the table and grinned. "Well, maybe one."

She giggled and faced him. "I think I can handle him. If he plays his cards right, that is."

Jake shook his head, backing her into the hallway. "I don't want to play cards."

"Oh yeah?" She stood on tiptoes, slipping her arms around his neck. "What do you want to do?"

He pressed his mouth against hers. "Why don't you use that imagination of yours?"

Joss smiled and returned the kiss.

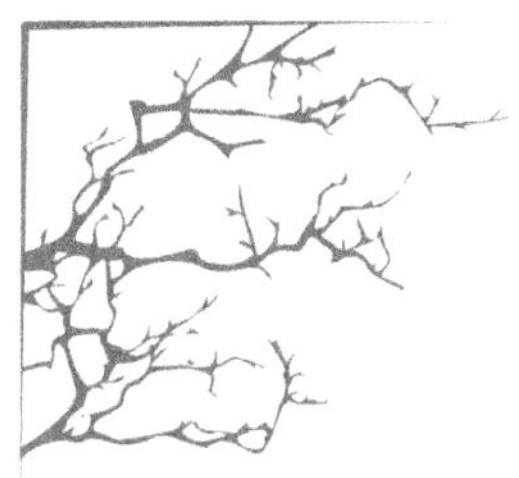

Chapter Five

AT SIX A.M. MONDAY morning Jake's alarm clock buzzed. He slapped it off, rubbed his eyes, and glanced around.

Joss slept soundly next to him. *No loud noises to disturb her.* She'd probably gotten her first good night's sleep in weeks.

I did, too. When he finally allowed sleep to take him he was relaxed, and more content than ever in his memory.

He rolled against her, kissing her neck. "Good morning."

"Not morning yet," she replied sleepily.

"Okay." He planted one more kiss on her nape, then moved away. "I have to go to work, anyway. You might as well sleep."

"Sleep, mmm..." She nestled into the pillow.

Jake grinned as he slid out of bed, tossing the covers over her sleeping form. He admired the view for a moment. Sprawled in his bed, hair tousled, softly snoring, she looked as sexy as ever. Unfortunately, he needed to spend tonight in her house looking for the source of that damnable noise. Hopefully, there'd be time for other things later. Shuffling to the bathroom, he closed the door behind him.

THERE WAS A WEEKLY meeting he needed to attend at the office and some paperwork to dispense. He briefed Taylor with the most pertinent details of Joss's case, then drank some coffee while making small talk with the other detectives. When nine a.m. rolled around he knew the lawyer's office should be open, so he phoned Joss on her cell.

"Hey there," she answered.

"Is it morning yet?" he teased.

"Barely. Where are you?"

"The office. I'd like you to call Roland Watkins about getting a copy of the will. If he doesn't want to play nice, I can get a subpoena. I don't imagine that'll be necessary."

"Okay. Should I say we'll pick it up?"

"You bet. Ask him what time this morning we can stop by, and call me back. If he balks, tell him to expect a call from the police."

"Oh, I love having muscle."

He chuckled, then spoke quietly into the phone, "What's left of my muscle, after that workout last night, is all yours."

"Mmm," she purred. "I hope you bounce back quickly. I had hopes for a repeat performance at some point."

"Me too." He glanced up as someone passed his desk. "I, uh—okay, call me back."

Joss chuckled. "I will."

He punched his phones *off* button, hoping Roland Watkins wouldn't cause trouble. The lawyer had to know any resistance would raise suspicion. Jake hadn't met him, but already didn't like the guy.

His phone rang, and he answered it quickly. "Gilford."

"Hey, Gilford," Joss said. "Watkins said no problem. Give his secretary twenty minutes to make a copy."

"Great. Here I was, worrying for no reason. I'll swing by to get you. How soon can you be ready?"

"Anytime. I'm about finished raiding your refrigerator."

"Find anything good?"

"Some yummy cinnamon-raisin bagels, but no tea. I'm having caffeine withdrawal."

"There's coffee."

"Not that desperate."

"There's no tea, that's a fact. Sorry."

"It's okay. I'll get some when we get to the house."

"You don't have to go, you know."

"Aw, Jake, I know you're trying to protect me, but I've got a lot to do. I need to finish going through my father's things, and I might as well do that while you're at work."

"Whatever you say. I'll be there in fifteen minutes or so."

"See you then." She smacked a kiss into the phone.

He smiled and hung up. Jake checked in with his boss and the clerk who kept track of detectives. He drove to his place, where Joss was waiting on the front porch swing.

"Hey." She climbed into his car and pressed a kiss to his cheek. "How's it going?"

"Not bad. I'm anxious to get a look at this will."

"You know where his office is?"

"Yeah, I looked it up." He drove to the lawyer's office, and Joss went inside. She returned a few minutes later with a large envelope stamped *legal document*. "Excellent." Jake leafed through the papers. "Let's go to the house. I want to go over this thoroughly."

"Sounds good to me."

At the mansion he settled on the sofa, will in hand. Joss fixed herself a glass of sweet tea and joined him. "You want anything?"

"No thanks," he replied, already reading. Wills were full of legal mumbo jumbo. He needed to get to the good stuff—the who, and what, of it all.

She sat in the chair next to him, picking up pages when he set them down. "Here we go." Jake waved a page in the air before reading from it, "All portions of the estate, including real estate, stocks, bonds and investments, are bequeathed to my sole heir, Jocelyn Renee Wheeler. In the event she precedes me in death, the estate goes to the charitable institution of *Save Our Wildlife*." He glanced up. "A charity? If you don't get it, the money goes to charity?"

"Wow," she murmured. "A nice gesture. Suppose a crazed gazelle somewhere is trying to off me?"

"It seems unlikely." He grabbed his pen, making notes. "*Save Our Wildlife*. I've never heard of it. I'll need to check it out."

"You think it's a bogus charity?"

"Don't know. It's a place to start, though. Let me go through the rest of this."

She nodded while he continued reading. There was nothing unusual in the last pages of the will. Roland Watkins was named executor, with one of his associates as the legal counsel. There was some legal jargon about why Watkins couldn't do both—conflict of interest, blah, blah, blah—and a breakdown of fees for each position.

They seemed in line with the little Jake knew about wills. He'd handled his own father's estate, and before that, helped sort out some legal stuff when his mother died. His parents were simple folk, so there hadn't been much to divvy up. Edward Cooper's estate easily ran to the millions.

"Hmm." He set the last sheet down and rubbed his eyes. "Interesting. I've got some research to do. I don't suppose you have a laptop?"

"Sorry." She shook her head. "I've got a computer at home, but don't use it that much."

"You're kidding. I'd go nuts without mine."

Joss shrugged, smiling sheepishly.

He stood and grinned at her. Leaning down to kiss her neck, he said, "I'm going to take off for a while. I'd like to take the will with me, see what digging I can do."

"It's all yours."

Jake glanced around. "Actually, it's all yours. Stuffed bobcat, elk antlers and all."

"Um, yeah, about that. Can you look up someone who might want to buy that stuff? If I can't sell it, I'll pitch it in the garbage, but I might as well try to make a buck."

"Like you really need it," he teased.

She laughed, shaking her head.

"I'll work on it. Will you be okay here for lunch? I can take you out to dinner."

"There's some pizza left over. I can eat that for *dinner*," she corrected. "You can take me out to supper."

"Southerners." He rolled his eyes, grinning. "I'll see you later. Think about what you want for *supper*."

"Yes, sir." She saluted him, eyes twinkling.

He paused to admire her for a moment, winked, then left.

JAKE PUSHED THE CHAIR back from his desk and stood up to stretch his legs. Several hours had passed while he surfed the Internet. When the office was quiet, he barely noticed the passage of time. Now his legs were cramped, his back stiff.

He went to the coffee pot and poured himself a cup. It was bitter, but he needed the pick-me-up. He hadn't stopped to eat once he hit on the information he was looking for.

There were several buyers in the Kansas City metro area for Joss's animal menagerie. If she wanted to, she could bargain for the best price. He'd take her the information he printed out. She could make some calls and decide.

There was plenty of information online regarding Kansas law pertaining to wills. It wasn't illegal for the lawyer to be executor of an estate, but it wasn't considered the best move. A separate lawyer and executor were usually prudent, and in everyone's best interest. Of course, each person would take a percentage of the estate, usually three to seven percent, before the funds were distributed.

Save Our Wildlife was a bit harder to pin down. They were based in Florida, if the post office box address on their meager website was accurate. The site listed three names as officers. Ross Whitcomb and William Rust had extensive profiles on the Internet. Jake's search engine pulled up several articles on each of them. Mostly business news, the men kept busy and appeared legitimate, involved in several Florida outfits. He never saw them mentioned in conjunction with *Wildlife*, but that didn't necessarily raise a red flag.

The third man, Eugene Tuttle, was more of a mystery. Searching for him on the web was futile. Even *Google* turned up nothing. Jake made notes on the items he wanted to follow up on, and Tuttle was definitely one of them.

The main thing that bothered him about the charity's website was the lack of information explaining what they actually did. There were pictures of animals, suggestions of ways to help animals, even a *click here* button for someone chomping at the bit to make a donation. But nowhere did it say what *Save Our Wildlife* would do with a person's hard-earned money.

Jake tossed his paper cup and stretched. Tomorrow, he'd make some calls and delve deeper into the charity. *So-called charity*. He wasn't sure he was convinced. One and one didn't add up to two in this case. He had to find the person behind the organization. *Unless there really is a crazed gazelle trying to off Joss.*

He smiled to himself, checked out for the day, and drove to her place. His stomach rumbled, and he wondered where she might like to eat. There were several good restaurants close by. He wasn't picky, just hungry. He knocked loudly before entering the foyer of the big house. "Hello?"

"Where in the devil have you been?" Joss screeched.

Jake ducked as a hardback book whizzed past his head.

Chapter Six

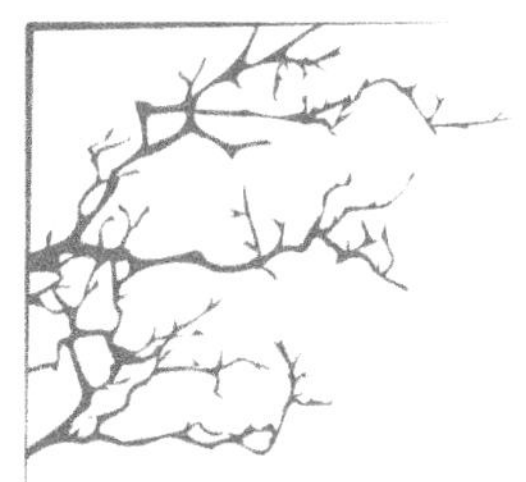

"WHAT ARE YOU DOING?" He covered his head with his arms as a second book found its mark, hitting his wrist.

"I've had it!" she stormed, stomping around the room.

"Joss, what is it?" Jake tried to follow, reaching for her, but she evaded him.

"You said you'd be back. I've been waiting here for you." Her voice was steely.

He stepped in front of her, shocked at what he saw. Her hair stood out, frizzy and wild. Glazed, glassy eyes stared back at him. He'd seen her like this one other time, agitated, but not as angry. "Sweetheart," he said carefully. "I said I'd be back for dinner—supper—whatever you call it. The evening meal."

"That was a week ago!" She took a swing at him, arm flailing wildly.

He dodged her fist. "Joss... Jocelyn... What are you talking about? I left you here this morning."

"It was a week ago, you bastard, and I'm not going to stand for your shit!" She swung at him with both arms, and he grabbed her. She continued to struggle, but he easily overpowered her, wrapping her in his arms.

"Hey, settle down." He spoke soothingly in her ear, "Joss, baby, stop."

She turned her head and made a motion to bite him.

"Stop that!" he commanded, pulling his face back. When he squeezed her arms, she drooped.

He leaned in carefully, speaking with forced calm reserve. "Don't bite me."

"I'm so tired of being used," she muttered. "Men make promises and never follow through."

"I've only been gone a few hours. I left you here this morning. We got the will, came here, read it…" He saw confusion on her face as she seemed to try and focus. "Remember? When I left, I said I'd be back to take you out to eat. That was this morning."

Joss closed her eyes, took several deep breaths. "This morning?"

"Yes." He exhaled a small sigh of relief, loosened his grasp on her. "Have you eaten anything?"

"I had some crackers."

"That's it? No pizza?"

She shook her head, then rubbed her hands over her face.

"Did you take anything? Something to help you relax, maybe?"

She shot him a dirty look. "I don't do drugs, Jake."

"I wasn't talking about illegal drugs. Maybe you have a prescription for something, like Valium, to help you relax?"

"Nothing. I haven't taken anything, I swear. I'm just so tired."

"Sit." He led her to the sofa and eased her onto it.

"I'm sorry." She seemed truly remorseful. "I don't know what came over me. It seemed like you'd been gone for days. I was so disoriented and terrified."

He sat beside her, pulling her into his arms. "Better now?"

"Yes." She nodded, snuggling into his chest. "I'm sorry, Jake."

"It's okay." He kissed the top of her head. "You had me scared, there, for a minute."

She looked up at him. "Did I hurt you?"

He rubbed her cheek gently. Her eyes were focused again and they looked clearer. Something was not right. "Nope. I was just worried about you."

"I'm fine. I hate being such a bother." She nestled into his chest.

"So, all you've had today is crackers… and tea?"

She slowly looked up again. "What are you saying?"

"I don't know, babe. Crackers are pretty tame. I'm wondering about that tea."

"Don't be ridiculous! My mother made it, for goodness sake."

"Okay, okay." He rubbed a hand over her head, trying to keep her calm. "My mind's always buzzing with possibilities."

"Hmph," she snorted. "Maybe you should focus on dinner. I'm starved."

"Me, too." He'd forgotten his hunger in the hubbub. Unsure if he really wanted to take her out in public after that outburst, he suggested, "What if we just finish that pizza?"

"That's fine. I don't feel like going out anyway."

He dragged her petite form onto his lap. Cradling her face, he asked, "Are you sure you're okay? For a minute there..." *You looked whacked out, and it scared the hell out of me.* He shook his head. "Let's just say, I was concerned."

"I'm fine. I'm so sorry, Jake. It must be the stress of..." she looked around the room, "all this."

"That must be it." He couldn't resist pressing his lips to hers. They shared a warm, lingering kiss.

She slipped her arms around his neck, returning the embrace with ardor.

Jake caressed her back and shoulders, thinking how easy it would be to roll her over on the sofa and lose himself in passion.

But something wasn't right, and he couldn't ignore it. In a short amount of time, Joss had come to mean a lot to him—more than a quick roll in the hay. The *"L"* word floated in the back of his mind. He couldn't speak it aloud, yet, but he thought he might *love* her.

He definitely had the urge to protect her, to solve all her problems. That other urge had him wanting to hold her in his arms twenty-four hours a day. *Could it be love?* He thought it could, secretly hoped it was. There was something mysterious and very appealing about Jocelyn Wheeler. He wouldn't mind spending fifty or sixty years figuring out what it was.

But first he had to deal with their immediate problems. He intended to have one of her special tea bags examined at the police lab. It seemed the obvious place to start. She'd been lucid and fine at his house. Once she got back here and drank that tea, the strange behavior started again.

He wouldn't mention it to her just yet. He didn't think she'd noticed the abnormal behavior before today. Today's performance was hard to miss.

If it wasn't the tea—well, he'd cross that bridge when he came to it. If she was schizophrenic or bipolar, those conditions could be helped with medication. If she was simply a nut, he'd have some decisions to make. That was for later, too. *Nothing to worry about yet.* At the moment, all he had to worry about was prying his body away from her enticing grasp so they could warm up some pizza.

HE WAS TORN. *Stay in the house searching for the source of the noise, or take Joss back to my place?* He wasn't sure she was strong enough to handle another round of ear-splitting clamor. Her mood was better, but she seemed fragile, and he hated to take the chance of upsetting her. On the other hand, he worried about leaving her alone.

It was an agonizing decision, one he wouldn't have had to make if he hadn't gotten personally involved. Unfortunately, he had a history of not being able to keep business and pleasure separate. He met the first woman he ever truly loved after her husband beat her up, almost killed her. She'd called the police; he and his partner had taken Lucy, and her two small children, to an emergency shelter, then hauled the husband to jail.

Two tumultuous years followed. Frank Walker served six months in prison, but never loosened his grip on Lucy. Jake tried to help her start a new life, settling her and the precious little children he'd grown to love into a nice rental house. He spent all his time and most of his discretionary income on the family, but he was happy to do it. For a while, they were happy, too.

When Frank got out on parole he returned, ostensibly, to see the kids. Suddenly, he was the best father and the most remorseful husband on the face of the earth. Jake saw the man working Lucy, reminding her of the good times, piling on layers of guilt for breaking up their family.

Jake suggested it was Frank who'd caused the break up by beating her every night, and was shocked when Lucy defended the jerk. *He only hit her when he was drunk*, she insisted, and he'd gotten sober in prison. He'd changed, she was sure of it.

There wasn't a cop alive who hadn't seen it before. Jake knew Frank hadn't changed. Something would eventually provoke him, he'd take a drink, and the beatings would resume. Lucy would put up with it until he seriously hurt one of the children, or he killed her. Jake couldn't make her see it. She was plagued with insecurities, blind to the deception before her eyes.

After many long nights of arguments, in a heart-wrenching decision, Jake let her go. Saying goodbye to the children was hardest of all. They had finally gotten over being scared all the time. Their blue eyes no longer looked frightened, but happy when he was around. He hated leaving them.

Frank found a job in another state, made arrangements with his parole officer, and moved the family away. It took a solid year for Jake's heart to heal after they left. He often thought about tracking them down, making sure they were all right. Finally, he forced himself to forget them. They weren't his family—or his problem—anymore.

He looked at Joss, curled up in the chair across from him. *Was he opening himself up for more heartache?* Her life was complicated. She came with a truckload of baggage, for sure. Perhaps he needed to lighten his load.

There was a cute little temp-secretary at the department, with long blond hair, a nicely filled out sweater, and legs that went on forever. Maybe he needed someone like that for a change. No history or drama, just some good, simple fun.

Joss stretched and straightened her leg, nudging him with her toe. "What are you so quiet for? You seem all introspective or something."

He glanced at her messy hair and tired eyes. In the time he'd known her, she hadn't shown much concern about her appearance. Most women ran off to check themselves in the mirror every so often, but she didn't seem to care. He liked that about her.

There were other things he liked, some obvious, some he couldn't quite put his finger on. She was different. Something about her tugged at him like no one ever had before. *I don't want simple. I want Joss.*

Running a finger over her toes, he said, "I think we should go back to my place. You need to rest."

She scooted down in her chair so he had better access to her foot. "That feels good. More, please."

"Want me to rub your feet?" He drew his finger behind the toes, causing them to curl.

"To begin with. Then maybe you could rub a few other places."

He traced an imaginary line down the arch of her foot. "That might be arranged. If you're up to it."

Joss wiggled her toes. "How about you? Are *you* up to it?"

He grinned, pressing small kisses to the tip of each toe. "I'll definitely be up to it. But we need to leave. I'm not doing anything here."

"I thought you planned to stay here tonight. Didn't you say—?"

"I know what I said," he cut her off, suddenly very interested in her wiggling toes and the effect they were having on him. "I changed my mind. We'll go back to my place tonight. I don't want to leave you alone."

"I don't want to be alone." She gazed into his eyes. "I want to be with you, Jake. I don't care where we are. When you wrap me in your arms, you take me to a whole new place. A place I've only been to with you."

He kissed her curved instep, watched her foot flex to his ministrations. "Feels a little like burying your head in the sand, doesn't it? We can't ignore real life forever."

"Is this place real?" She glanced around. "I didn't know my father and so far I haven't discovered anything here that has me mourning his loss. This house is totally strange."

"I'd tend to agree. However, I think you need to uncover everything you can before you form opinions." He nipped at the soft pad of flesh before her heel, and she jumped. "But not tonight. Tonight, we can bury our heads in the sand—or somewhere equally warm and inviting—for a while longer."

Joss groaned and flopped back into her chair. "Don't make me move. I'm comfortable right here. Besides, if you keep doing that thing with my foot, I won't be able to walk. My knees are already wobbly."

He lowered her foot and stood up. Offering a hand to help her to her feet, he said, "Let's go. We can be at my place in a few minutes."

"Not soon enough," she grumbled, but allowed him to pull her up. He guided her by the waist, stopping only for her shoes and purse before he ushered her out the door.

JAKE HELD THE FLUFFY bath towel out, wrapping it around Joss as she climbed from the tub. His house was modern, but he was a sucker for the big, old claw-footed tub, roomy enough for two. When he discovered it at an estate sale, he'd snapped it up and installed it himself.

Not that he'd had much opportunity to put it to good use. His last few relationships were brief and to the point. He hadn't spent a lot of time lounging in the tub with any of his recent love interests.

Joss, now she was someone he could lounge with. He envisioned long soaks with her after work, sipping wine, unwinding, talking about their days. It sounded just about perfect.

He ran one finger over a tiny cut on her lower lip. "You bit your lip. I thought I tasted blood." He kissed the small wound.

She smiled lazily, wrapping her hands around his neck. "I can't be held responsible for anything that happens when you make love to me. Sometimes I feel like it's not even me. I'm outside my body, looking down at one lucky, lucky woman."

"Oh, it's you, all right." He clutched her to him. "I feel that, too, Joss. Something incredible—indescribable—happens when we're together. I can't explain it, but I know I love it." It might have been the intensity of the moment, or one of another thousand feelings that raced through him, but he found himself murmuring, "I love *you*."

Joss smiled, reached for his face and lowered it to hers. "I love you, too, Jake. And I'd love to stay here and talk about it all night, but I just realized I'm starving!"

He chuckled. "Such a romantic. Come on." They each threw on one of his robes and wandered to the kitchen, raiding the refrigerator for sustenance. Over cold chicken and greasy fried wontons, they talked nonstop. "First girlfriend?" she asked, nibbling a wing.

"Donna Martin, third grade. She had braces. I thought they were so cool."

"Oh my gosh!" Joss laughed. "First *serious* girlfriend, you know. Time and place."

"Oh, the first time I *did it*? Lord. That would have been after the Jackson Heights football game. We won, and I was pumped."

"You played? What position?"

"Are we still talking sex here?"

She swatted his arm, and they chuckled. "Okay," he continued. "I played quarterback for two years."

"Did you play in college?"

"Nah, I knew what I wanted to do. College football required a commitment I wasn't prepared to invest. It was fun in high school, though."

"So back to the Jackson Heights game. You won, and—?"

"And Marcy Sharvis was the head cheerleader. She had this short little skirt, a really tight sweater, and these pom poms..."

"Oh no!" She squealed. "Did she keep her uniform on?"

"Part of it, I shoved the skirt up. But we had to lose the sweater, you know. It's a guy thing. We used the pom poms for a pillow in the back seat of my Chevy, so her head was surrounded by these blue and white wispy puffs. I can still remember how she looked, lying there. Course, she wasn't there for very long. It was my first time and all."

Joss broke into peals of laughter, holding her stomach.

He grinned. "Fortunately for you, I've developed self-control over the years."

"Thank you!" She managed to get out, still laughing.

"Okay, you next. First time, who and where."

She gulped some water and wiped tears from her eyes. "You crack me up. I don't have nearly as funny of a story to tell. Mark Williams, in college. We went out, he got me drunk, drove me to a secluded spot. He had a small car, so he threw a blanket out on the ground. That's about all I can remember, except how much it hurt. I cried, he was pissed because he didn't, you know, and he drove me home. I never saw him again."

Jake's face tightened. "Did you call anyone? Report him?"

She shrugged. "For what? He didn't rape me. I thought it seemed like a good idea at the time, but apparently he didn't have the finesse to pull it off. There wasn't much good about it, but it was mutual."

"I hate that story. Tell me a better one."

"I'm not giving you a list of the guys I've been with. There aren't that many, but it feels a little weird, Jake."

"You started this line of questioning. The last one, then. Who was your last boyfriend, and why did you break up?"

"That's easy. I can do that. Fred Deane, a guy from the restaurant where I worked. Great big hulking black guy. You'd have thought a man with such God-given gifts might have known how to use his assets a little better. He was pathetic!"

They laughed again. Jake was relieved. He liked to see her happy, not melancholy.

Joss wiped her hands on a napkin and moved behind him, slipping her arms around his neck. She laid her head on the back of his shoulder. "I'm not going to ask about your last girlfriend. I might not like it. I should warn you, I have this little jealous streak."

He leaned back into her. "Good to know. You've got nothing to worry about, beautiful. I'm faithful to the core, a real one-woman man. And it excites me to think that you're my one woman."

"Me too, baby," she said softly, rocking against him. "I just wish that other stuff was behind us. I'm afraid to go back to the house, Jake. Something's not right there. It frightens—no, terrifies me."

He moved one hand to cover hers. "You don't have to go back. I've decided to enlist some help from the department, to get things over with faster. I'll make arrangements tomorrow. But you should stay here. Don't go back, Joss."

"I won't," she agreed, hugging him. "I'll stay right here."

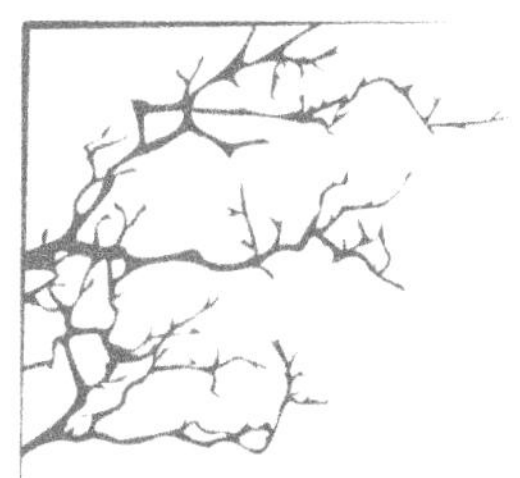

Chapter Seven

JAKE TUGGED UNCOMFORTABLY at the collar of his shirt. Even after eight years on the police force, he'd never gotten used to wearing neckties. There was no getting around it in the uniformed division, but once he became a detective, he saved ties for special, or necessary, occasions.

He always wore a suit coat and kept a tie stuffed in the pocket just in case. A sharply dressed detective with a badge clipped to his jacket usually achieved better results than a laid-back one. Jake fidgeted with the tie again. Roland Watkins hadn't sounded pleased to take his phone call, even less thrilled to make an appointment to meet. The lawyer seemed to be playing head games, making him wait.

From his seat in the outer office, Jake could see through the glass window panel beside the front door. In the hallway hung a plaque with a directory of people who had office space on that floor. Of the twenty names listed, one jumped out at him. Eugene Tuttle.

Where have I heard that name? The memory escaped him. It was an unusual last name. Jake chuckled, remembering Tuttle on the old TV series *M*A*S*H*. Trapper and Hawkeye had invented the man as a lark. He never existed, but everyone insisted they knew him. Captain Tuttle, the invisible man.

"Mr. Gilford? Mr. Watkins will see you now." The brunette behind the desk rose, leading the way to the inner sanctum of the office.

"Thank you." Jake tried to ignore the woman's tight fitting skirt, but each sway of her hips made it difficult.

The secretary opened the main office door and held it, requiring Jake to squeeze past her. She smelled sweet, like bubble gum mixed with a rose-scented perfume. Her gaze seemed to admire him as she said, "Here you go. Mr. Watkins, this is Mr. Gilford."

Jake smiled, letting his gaze roam over her quickly. "Thanks again, uh—"

"Betty," she supplied, batting her lashes.

"Thanks, Betty." She appeared to appreciate his attention, and he hoped he boosted her morale. *If it made her feel good...* Hell, it made him feel good, too. Besides, he might need her help in the future.

She slipped out, and he turned to the lawyer seated behind the desk. Roland Watkins signed paper after paper, apparently hoping Jake would go away.

He cleared his throat and stepped forward, trying tact first. "Mr. Watkins, I'm Jake Gilford, a detective with the KCPD. We spoke on the phone, and I mentioned that I'm helping Jocelyn Wheeler settle her father's estate."

The lawyer stopped writing and raised his eyes. "Of course. Hello, Mr. Gilford. Have a seat." He motioned to the two chairs in front of his desk.

Jake smiled at the man, taking in his appearance as he sat. Watkins, probably fifty years old, had thick dark hair slicked back with gel. He was tan and seemed fit. Jake guessed him to be a golfer. A man didn't get that tanned walking to and from his car. "Actually, it's *Detective Gilford*. I'm with David Taylor's outfit. I believe you know him."

Watkins didn't bat an eye. "Yes, I know him, he's a good man."

"He was a friend of Edward Cooper."

"An old friend, perhaps. Edward didn't socialize much in his later years."

"Why is that?" Jake leaned back, crossing his legs. "Poor health?"

"He suffered from prostate cancer for the last five years of his life. After his first surgery he was in remission for a few years. His symptoms reappeared, and the doctor found the cancer had metastasized to his lungs. Nothing could be done at that point. Edward died nine months later."

"Nine months." Jake mulled that over. "Do you know why he didn't try to contact his daughter earlier? If he had, they might have had the opportunity to at least meet."

"Edward had conflicted feelings about the girl. He didn't plan to contact her at all. I convinced him it would be the best thing, since she's his sole heir. He could go to meet his maker knowing he'd done what he needed to do."

"You convinced him," Jake repeated, trying to keep the skepticism from his voice. He highly doubted this version of events, but no one could refute it.

"Of course. He harbored feelings of guilt. He never felt like he did enough for the girl. This was the least he could do."

Jake snorted. "Leaving her everything he owned is a lot more than the *least* he could do, Mr. Watkins. According to the will, the estate is valued in the millions."

Watkins shrugged, an insincere smile pasted on his face. "He never knew his daughter, Detective. Edward suffered miserably because of that."

"Really?" Jake paused to mull the statement over. *Suffered miserably?* He saw an easy fix for that. All Edward Cooper had to do was pick up the phone and call Joss. They might have had their reunion long before the man kicked off.

The lawyer stood up and moved to a small table at the side of the office. From a carafe, he poured coffee into one mug, took a sip, and returned to his desk.

"I'm good, thanks." Jake waved a hand.

"Sorry, Detective. I thought we were about done here. You have more questions?"

"Yes, I do." Jake uncrossed his legs, pulled the notebook from his jacket pocket. He read from it for a moment then said, "*Save Our Wildlife.* What can you tell me about them?"

"Edward contributed to them at the highest level. He was very interested in the cause of animals."

"Interested in hunting them, that's pretty obvious," Jake added. "But why would he care enough to leave them millions? I find that rather incredible."

Watkins settled back into his chair. "Edward was concerned about the humane treatment of animals. He hunted, but he was ethical and followed the rules. Besides, he didn't leave them millions, Detective Gilford. Miss Wheeler gets the money, remember?"

"I remember. But the funny thing is, someone's trying to scare Miss Wheeler out of the house. Strange things are happening there. That's how I became involved."

Watkins' phone buzzed. He ignored it, staring at Jake, who continued, "It's not going to work, though. I don't scare as easily as Miss Wheeler. We'll figure it out, or just sell the house, makes little difference to me. She'll get her money either way."

Another buzz had Watkins glancing at his phone. He frowned before saying, "Excuse me." Punching the red flashing button, he spoke into the receiver, "Yes? Okay, put him on." He swiveled in his chair, his back toward Jake. "What is it, Devon? I'm in a meeting."

Jake paid attention to the one-sided conversation.

"Why can't you use their van? Oh, I see. I suppose you can use the truck. The keys are hanging in the mud room. Devon—drive carefully, and don't leave the gas tank on empty, please. Okay, I'll see you." He rotated back to face Jake, replacing the receiver. "Sorry about that. Kids."

"Ah, I love kids." Jake smiled. "What does your son do?"

"He works at Starlight Music. They provide disc jockey services for all kinds of events, wedding receptions, parties, whatever. They're supposed to have their own van to haul equipment, but lately it's been *in* the repair shop more than out."

"That'd be a very interesting line of work. I bet they use all kinds of electronic gadgets in a job like that."

"They do. In fact…" Watkins hesitated, appearing as if he'd said too much. He refocused and stated, "Enough about that. You have more questions? I really must get back to work."

"Just a few." Jake glanced at what he'd jotted in his notebook. *Save Our Wildlife*, corporation officers Ross Whitcomb, William Rust and Eugene Tuttle. *Eugene Tuttle!* That's where he'd heard the name. Someone had used that name to rent an office on the same floor as Watkins, in this building. *What a coincidence.* "Have you ever heard of Ross Whitcomb?"

Watkins thought about it. "Can't say that I have."

"What about William Rust?"

Another blank look. "Sounds familiar, but I can't place him. Sorry."

"Eugene Tuttle?"

"Nope," Watkins answered, a little too quickly.

"Are you sure about that? Eugene Tuttle? The sign in the hallway says he has an office on this floor."

"There are a dozen offices on this floor, Detective. My partners and I have eight employees right here in our own suite of offices. I wouldn't begin to keep track of who else comes and goes in the building."

"Really, not even here on the same floor? You haven't met him in the elevator perhaps?"

Watkins simply stared at him.

"I guess not. You see, I'm trying to figure out who the brains are behind *Save Our Wildlife*. They stand to inherit a bundle if something happens to Joss—Miss Wheeler. Of course, I intend to see that nothing happens to her."

"Of course." The lawyer stood, extended his hand. "Good luck, Detective. If I can be of further help, just call."

Jake took his time leaving. He stood, shook hands with Watkins, and slowly exited the office. Watkins watched him impatiently, which caused Jake to move even slower.

In the outer office, he stopped in front of the secretary's desk. "Betty, do you know Eugene Tuttle? The directory in the hall says he has an office on this floor."

She squinted and thought about it. "I don't believe I do. I know most of the people on the floor. We share the elevator several times a day."

Exactly as I suspected. They'd become familiar with faces, then names, and would eventually know most of the people in offices around them.

"Some folks rent offices, but never move in," Betty continued. "I've seen that several times in this building. Not sure why, though."

"Who would I talk to, to find out if Mr. Tuttle ever moved in?"

She rifled through her desk drawer and pulled out a business card. "MDP Management handles the leases and maintenance on this building. Ask for Susie, she's a friend of mine. Tell her I sent you."

"Thanks, Betty." Jake smiled at her. He took the card and headed for the door. In the hallway, he punched the phone number from the card into his cell phone.

"MDP Management, Renee speaking," a woman answered.

"May I speak with Susie, please?"

"One moment." While she placed him on hold, he paced the hallway, looking at suite names and numbers. The directory indicated Tuttle's office in suite 415, but the door there had no sign. Not that the man was even the same Eugene Tuttle as on the *Wildlife* website, but Jake suspected one hell of a coincidence.

"This is Susie," announced a voice on the line.

"Susie, hi. This is Detective Jake Gilford with the Kansas City Police Department. I got your number from Betty, at the law offices of Roland Watkins and Associates."

"Sure! What can I do for you, Detective?"

"I see the name of Eugene Tuttle on the directory here, same floor as Watkins. What can you tell me about him?"

"Eugene Tuttle," she repeated. "Let me check."

He heard computer clicks and beeps.

"Tuttle signed the lease six months ago, for two years."

"Suite 415?"

"Yes."

He moved down the hall. "That's what the directory says, but I don't see any signs of life in 415. I'm in front of the door now. There's no name or anything."

"Evidently, he hasn't moved in yet."

"After six months? Isn't that strange? I can't imagine the rent is cheap here."

She chuckled. "No, it's not. But it's not that strange. Sometimes people start a business, which doesn't work out. Then there are people who rent space to have an address, but never actually move in. We don't like that, but it happens."

"Tuttle hasn't contacted you to get out of his lease?"

"Not that I'm aware of. I'm sure I'd know. I handle the accounts."

"Do you know if he gets mail here?"

"I don't. We wouldn't know that. The post office might be able to help you."

"Okay, thanks, Susie. I appreciate it."

"You bet, anytime."

He snapped his phone shut, shoved it in his pocket. *Next stop—post office.*

The post office clerk was not as forthcoming with information as she could have been, Jake decided. He tossed a few names around, and had to mention getting a subpoena before the woman agreed to look up the address. Mail for Eugene Tuttle's office had indeed been forwarded to a post office box, number 272, located in the substation where they stood. Security cameras covered all the boxes, but to see the tapes would require a court order.

Jake hummed as he returned to the department. He could get a court order. A long shot, but a risk he felt worth taking. Something about *Save Our Wildlife* smelled fishy. He smiled at his own pun.

He arranged for the court order, then touched base with the members of the surveillance unit scheduled to meet him at the mansion for the night. Confident their plan was in place, he signed out mid-afternoon. He'd be working all night; he wanted to take some time off before then.

He found Joss asleep on the sofa when he arrived home. He sat on the edge next to her hip, ran a hand over her hair. "Hey, sleeping beauty. I'm home."

She stretched, yawned, but didn't open her eyes. "Prince Charming?"

"Yep, that's me. If you keep your eyes closed, that is."

She smiled and opened them. "No way. I love looking at you. I could look at you all day long."

He leaned in, pressing a light kiss to her lips. "Gee, that sounds boring. I could think of many more interesting ways to pass the time."

Joss slid her arms around his neck. "Tell me some."

His mouth moved to her neck. "Do you really want to talk? Cause I can talk, if you like."

She covered his mouth with her hand. "Don't talk. Kiss. Keep kissing, don't stop."

He smirked and kissed his way around her neck until he reached her other ear. "Why don't we move this party to the bedroom? We can spread out, get more comfortable."

"I'd love that, Jake, but I'm so tired. I'm not sure I can move."

Pulling back to look at her, he frowned. "Are you okay?"

"Yeah." She smiled, caressing his face lovingly.

Jake gazed into her eyes. She'd been lucid since he brought her here, but now, something wasn't right.

She hiccupped and grabbed her mouth, eyes widening.

"You okay?"

"No!" Still holding her mouth, Joss made a gagging sound, and Jake rolled off in an instant. "Oh, no!" she muttered, running for the bathroom.

Right behind her, he watched her kneel in front of the toilet and throw up. She retched twice more, then sat on the floor. Jake grabbed a washcloth, wet it, and pressed it to her forehead.

"I'm sorry." She sat back, clutching the washcloth to her mouth.

"No, I'm the one who should be sorry. I didn't realize kissing me might make you sick."

"Would you stop with the teasing, already?" she muttered crankily.

"I'm sorry, Joss. Just trying to make you feel better."

"I need sleep. That's all it is. I'm so tired."

"I wish you'd said something." His voice sounded irritable now, and he knew it. "If you felt that tired, I would have never started anything."

"Don't snap at me!" She stood, washed her face at the sink, then rinsed her mouth.

"I wasn't snapping. What is up with you?"

"That's not snapping?" Joss marched from the bedroom to the kitchen. She threw open the refrigerator and pulled out a pitcher.

"What is that?" He followed, even more irritated.

"What do you think it is? Sweet tea, same as I always drink." She grabbed a glass and poured the tea into it. She downed half of it.

His mind raced. When he'd removed the tea bag to take it to the lab, he thought it'd been the last one. She must have had another. *Damn it!* Apparently, she'd brought it with her at the same time she picked up her car and a suitcase full of clothes. "Take it easy on that stuff. I think it's making you sick."

"You're full of it. I've been drinking my mama's sweet tea since I was a baby." She eyed him defiantly and drained her glass.

"Okay, you know best." He raised his hands, turned, and strolled off to the bedroom. He changed and glanced at his watch. He had some time to kill before meeting the team at seven. He'd see if Joss was hungry, and grab a bite to eat before going back to the mansion.

Joss crawled into his bed and burrowed under the covers.

He stood beside her, wanted to reach out, but didn't. "Will you be okay?"

"Yes. Go away, Jake."

"I assume you don't want anything to eat."

"Go away!" She covered her head with a pillow.

Frustration washed over him, but he held his tongue. Unsure what to say, he headed for the door, grabbed his jacket and keys, then left.

"Jake," she called after him.

He stopped and looked back. "Yeah?"

Joss peered at him with glassy, frightened eyes. "Fix this."

"I will," he assured her with more confidence than he felt. Positive he could fix the house, praying he could fix her.

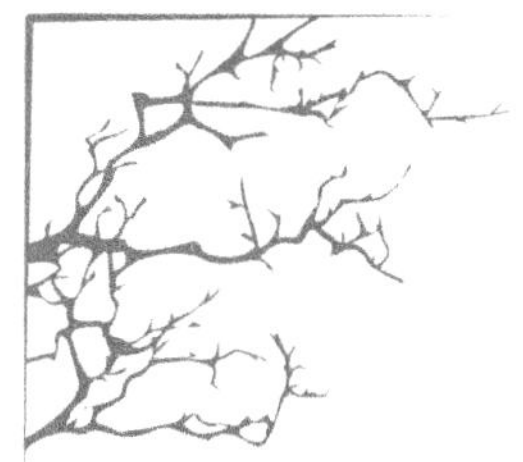

Chapter Eight

THE SURVEILLANCE TEAM arrived sharply at seven p.m. They wanted some daylight to search the house before the show started. Jake watched them enter, man after man, carrying briefcases loaded with special equipment. "Man," he muttered to Roy, the group leader, shaking his head. "You have more gadgets than those *Ocean's Thirteen* guys."

"Of course, we do." Roy grinned, teeth pearly gleamed white against his dark skin. He opened his briefcase, lined with techno-gadgets. "We're the good guys. We've got digital recorders, heat sensors, infrared lights, sound receivers...you name it. The only thing they got going for them is Julia Roberts."

"And George Clooney," one of Roy's team commented, stopping to give an exaggerated shake of his hips before moving on.

"Depends which way your door swings, I guess," Roy replied, winking at Jake.

"Hey, I like George Clooney," Jake joked.

Shaking his head, Roy shoved a box into Jake's hands. "Take this to Timmy upstairs."

"Which one is Timmy?"

"Walk up the stairs and say, 'Timmy?' He'll let you know."

"Yes, Boss." Jake did as Roy advised, and a big, burly fellow poked his head around the corner.

"Yep?"

"Here you go." He handed the box over.

"Thanks." Timmy disappeared.

Jake wandered from room to room. *These guys know their stuff.* Each of them went to work. They seemed to know exactly what to do, which impressed him. If this team didn't find something, there was nothing to be found.

They settled into position by eight-thirty, with Jake and Roy pacing the front room. "Who lived here?" the tall man asked, touching the head of the stuffed bobcat.

"Edward Cooper. Some big shot insurance investigator in his day. Apparently he loved hunting big game animals and spent his vacations on safaris in Africa and various places."

"His daughter inherited the place?"

"That's right."

Roy gave another glance around. "She as kooky as her old man?"

"Joss?" Merely mentioning her name caused Jake to smile. "No, she's great."

"Uh oh. I know that look. You're falling for her."

Jake scanned the room; they were alone. He lowered his voice. "Well, sort of."

"Sly dog." Roy chuckled. "This place is worth a bundle. You're making nice with the rich woman."

"No!" Jake muttered, shocked. That hadn't occurred to him. Of course, Joss would inherit money. That had nothing to do with how he felt about her. Obviously, it didn't appear that way from the outside. He tried to explain. "It's not like that. Joss is special. She's beautiful, smart, funny—"

Roy's radio crackled, and he held up a finger. "Roy here," he spoke into his collar microphone.

"Team One, checking in." Another voice followed, "Team Two, checking in." Then a third, "Team Three, all clear up here."

"Roger that. Out," Roy responded and looked at Jake. "It's eight-forty-five. We touch base on the quarter hour."

Jake nodded, still trying to defend himself. "It's really not like that, Roy."

The detective shrugged. "If you say so, man. No skin off my back."

"Tell me something," Jake said, his mind running through scenarios. "Maybe I'm being naïve, but I just keep wondering. Why would a wealthy white man have an affair with a black woman and, once he discovered she was pregnant, abandon her?"

Roy laughed. "Why wouldn't he? Did you hear yourself? Wealthy white man thinks he can do whatever the hell he pleases—he can do *whomever* the hell he pleases, for that matter. Black woman, probably poor, some type of service worker—"

"A waitress at the time, now she's a nurse."

Roy nodded. "Think about it, man. Most people are asshats."

"I just don't get it. How could a man ignore a kid he created?" Jake shook his head. "I could never do that, not in a million years."

"What do you see when you look at me?" Roy asked.

Jake shrugged. "A nice guy. Good cop. Hair's a little thin, so you shave it for that Michael Jordan look..." He grinned.

Roy laughed. "That's just you, Jake. Most people see a black man. Lots of folks are scared of me before they find out I'm a cop. They see a big, bald, black dude. But you just see the dude, don't you?"

He shrugged again. "I've always been that way. Make's a rat's hind end to me what color your skin is. Treat me right, and I'll treat you right."

Roy nodded, then said, "This Joss, she a dark-skinned girl?"

"Fairly. Her old man was white, so you know, medium."

"If you're going to be with her, you gotta expect prejudice. Some people aren't going to like her, or accept her...or her little nappy-headed kids. Cause even though they're half yours, the African-American in them is going to shine through. Count on it. There'll be people who won't like it. That's just the way life is."

"Not my life," Jake said simply.

Roy smiled. "She's a lucky woman."

The sound of a freight train barreled through the living room, and the men jumped. "Here we go!" Jake shouted.

"Stay close, but outta my way!" Roy bounded to the stairs.

Jake followed, and they tracked the source, ending up in Joss's room.

"It's in the ceiling!" one of the men shouted. The team focused their equipment there, all in agreement.

Jake watched each man test for something different. He recognized the sound receivers, heat sensors, and infrared lights, but many more of the devices, he didn't know.

Roy turned to him, yelling, "There might be an easier way to get to it, but the fastest way is to take out the ceiling. It'll be messy."

"Do it!" Jake yelled back.

As men moved into place and swung axes, Jake looked up at the ceiling. Sheetrock and dust poured down around them. Something white floated down the hallway. Jake caught a glimpse in his peripheral vision.

He ran to the doorway in time to see the white filmy vision ascend the stairs. Jake was torn—he glanced back to where the men had hoisted themselves up, searching the ceiling, and decided they could manage without him.

The train whistle sounded, almost piercing his eardrums. He raced for the stairs, took them by twos, and glanced around. He spotted one open bedroom door and decided to start there.

At the doorway, a blast of cold air hit him in the chest. He immediately saw that the third-floor window stood open. Rushing to it, he skidded to a stop as he noticed the apparition through the window. He rubbed his eyes and looked again.

Joss teetered on the edge of the sloped roof, three stories above the ground. She wore a billowy white nightgown that wafted around her ankles and bare feet. Her hands covered her ears.

"Jocelyn," he called carefully, anxious not to startle her. The concrete driveway circled in a wide span below, a long way down. If she fell, she couldn't miss it. *She won't fall.* He couldn't let her.

Leaning out the window, he shouted, "Hey!" The rumbling racket of the train made normal speech impossible.

She didn't face him. Standing on the slanted, uneven shingles of the old roof, Joss wavered. She wobbled, and his heart clutched.

"Joss!" he yelled at the same time the house went silent.

She whirled around, startled, and stared at him with sunken, glassy eyes. "What the—"

"Don't move!" he called, reaching for her.

"Jake!" She screamed, took a step, and fell.

He lunged out of the window in a desperate grab. He made contact with a handful of soft fabric—her nightgown. Hanging on with all his strength, he inched closer as the fabric made small ripping sounds. "Joss!" He didn't recognize the voice as his own. He froze, terrified—more frightened than he'd ever been in his life.

He couldn't see her. All he had was one handful of cotton. He reached over the windowsill, struggling to grab any body parts, an arm, a leg, anything. There was nothing.

The gown split, making another tearing sound—a noise much worse than anything the mansion had thrown at him so far. He inhaled, focused his energy and dove forward, capturing her foot.

"Joss!" Relief washed through him. He had her. They both might go out the window, but he would *not* let go.

"What the hell?" Roy hollered from behind him, and suddenly three men filled the space of the window.

Someone pulled Jake back into the room, while he still held her foot. Two officers lifted an unconscious Joss through the window.

He could have wept with relief. "Joss!" He scooped her into his arms, laying her gently on the bed. "Wake up."

She didn't respond.

"Timmy, call an ambulance," Roy ordered. "Tell them her breathing is erratic, we don't know much else."

Jake dropped to the bed next to her, feeling her pulse, checking her airway.

"She's breathing on her own, that's a good thing," Roy observed. "We'll keep her warm until the paramedics get here."

"Yeah," Jake agreed, pulling the coverlet off the opposite side of the bed and throwing it over her. He stared at her for a minute, remembering how frightened and disheveled she'd looked standing on the roof.

"What the hell was she doing?" Roy asked.

"She's sick." It was the only answer he could offer. The only justification he could find. *The tea bags.* He'd taken one to the lab yesterday. They told him it would take forty-eight hours for the results. He'd call them and put a rush on it. The Chief would call them if necessary. He needed to know the contents of that tea bag.

"You saved her life."

"I don't know about that." Jake hesitated. He couldn't allow himself to imagine what might have happened.

"You did." Roy put a hand on his shoulder. "I still say she's a lucky woman."

"Thanks." Jake stroked her forehead. In the distance, a siren wailed. It reminded him, and he glanced up. "Did you find anything in the ceiling?"

"Oh yeah!" Roy's face lit up. "The most sophisticated piece of sound equipment I've seen in a long time. It plays thirty tracks of music, or in this case, noise and sounds. A person can set the schedule, duration, whatever they want."

"That's it!" Jake marveled. Thrilled they discovered it, the *why* still loomed over him. "What's a piece of equipment like that normally used for?"

"It's essentially a programmable PA board. There are plenty of reasons someone would use one of these things. It might be used in a recording studio, or making the soundtrack to a movie. Hell, I can even see a DJ using it to set up a string of tunes at a dance."

"A DJ," Jake repeated, setting his jaw. Devon Watkins, the lawyer's son, worked for Starlight Music, a business that provided DJs for various events. *Isn't that an interesting coincidence?*

Two paramedics carried a gurney through the door, and Jake stood.

"Any change?" the female emergency technician asked, assessing Joss.

"No." He watched them move her, strap her to the back board, and take off.

"Which hospital are you taking her to?" He followed them to the ambulance.

"Mercy is closest," the woman replied as they climbed in.

He nodded. "I'll meet you there." Jake closed the big metal door and slapped it. The driver took off, lights and sirens blaring.

"I hope she's all right," Roy said.

"Thanks." Jake glanced around. "I need to get to the hospital."

"I'll handle the house. I'm taking the digital PA board to the station to test for fingerprints and anything else we might find."

"Sounds good. Thanks, Roy." Jake shook his hand. He made a dash for his car, tossed a portable, magnetic beacon light on top, then sped off. *Joss will be okay*, he repeated, over and over to himself. *She has to be okay.*

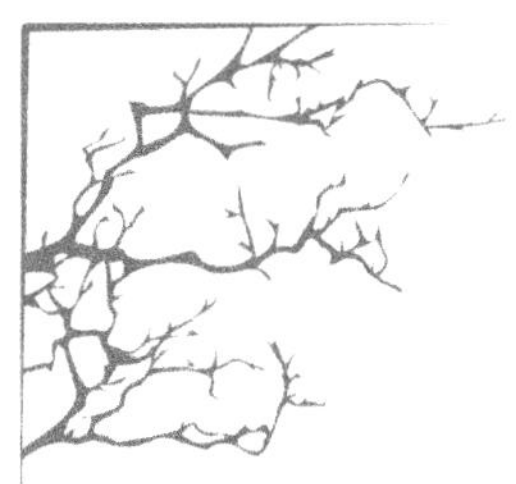

Chapter Nine

WHILE DOCTORS EXAMINED Joss at the hospital, Jake filled out the obligatory forms. Embarrassed, he realized how little he knew about her. He paced the halls for an hour, sipped coffee, and prayed to a God that hadn't heard much from him recently.

Finally, a doctor in scrubs entered the waiting room. "Jocelyn Wheeler?"

"Yes." Jake sprang from his chair.

"You family?"

He hesitated. "I'm her, uh, boyfriend."

The doctor glanced around. "No family here?"

Jake set his jaw. "I'm also a police detective, and she's a witness in a case we're working. You can tell me her condition."

The doctor frowned.

"I could make a phone call. Wake up a judge and get him to sign a court order. They're pretty friendly when we wake them in the middle of the night."

"I couldn't care less about your threats, Detective. But if you're close to the woman—"

He sighed. "I am. I'm sorry, Doc. It's been a long night. I'm extremely worried about her."

The doctor's face softened. "She's unresponsive. Her vitals are stable; we're not too concerned there. But it's why she's unconscious that's a mystery. We're running some tests to find out."

"She was drugged," Jake said without thinking. He had no proof, nothing to back up the statement, but he believed in his heart it was true. "She's acted strangely this past week, sometimes tired, sometimes almost manic. I took a special homemade tea bag of hers to the lab to be tested. I should get the results tomorrow."

"You really think that's it?"

"I'm convinced of it. She drank that tea nonstop, morning to evening."

"We need to know what the lab finds, the sooner the better. Any way to get those results sooner?"

"I'll call when the lab opens at eight."

"Make sure they realize it's a matter of life and death."

Jake's heart froze and he gulped. "I will. Can I see her?"

"For a few minutes. She's in the intensive care unit; visitors are allowed ten minutes every hour."

"Thank you." Jake followed the doctor to where Joss lay. Hooked up to monitors and machines, she looked small in a bed that really wasn't that large, her skin unnaturally pale. He sat beside her, grasped her hand, and held it to his cheek. "I'm here, baby. I know you can hear me. You've got to hang in there, Joss. Be strong. We'll figure out what's wrong; the doctors will make it better. I promised you I'd fix this. I promised..." He broke down, tears streaming down his face.

He couldn't remember the last time he'd cried, but at that moment, he didn't care. Jake buried his face in the bed, squeezing her hand. *I let you down.* She'd almost died because he hadn't handled things. He closed his eyes and sobbed.

SOMEONE TOUCHED HIS shoulder, and he jumped.

"Time to wake up," a nurse said gently.

"Wake up?" Jake bolted upright. His back kinked. *How long have I been leaning over the bed like that?* Morning sun streamed through the window. He glanced at Joss. She looked the same.

"Her condition is unchanged," the nurse offered.

Jake stood up and stretched his back.

"Sorry if your back is stiff, we let you sleep. We figured it was the best thing for both of you."

"I thought you had rules about ICU visitors."

"We do. But it was the middle of the night. The doctor went home. Besides, nurses run the hospital."

"Thank you." Jake smiled at her. "So, no change?"

"Nothing yet."

He checked his watch—seven-thirty—the lab opened at eight. He pulled a business card from his wallet and circled his cell number. "I'm going to leave for a while. If she wakes, or there's any change, could you please call me?"

"Sure, Detective. Does she have any family we can get in touch with?"

"Her mother's in New Orleans. I'll track down her number and call." He placed a kiss on Joss's forehead then headed home to shower and change.

His mind in a fog, he hoped a shower would help. It at least gave him time to make a mental list of things to do. He always worked better with a list.

With half a bagel and a cup of coffee in him, he dressed and searched the house for her cell phone, assuming her mother's number would be in it. He couldn't find Joss's purse, or her phone. They could be in her car, probably parked at the mansion. He hadn't noticed it last night, but it had to be there.

Jake drove to the house and found her car, unlocked. He rifled through it until he found her purse under the passenger's seat. The phone was there, and he searched through it for her mother's number. When he found it he hesitated then shut the phone off. He needed to call the lab and put a rush on the test results first. It'd be better to have something concrete to tell her mother, rather than the fact that Joss was simply unconscious for no reason. Hoping he'd made the right choice, he decided to wait and call her when he knew something.

Removing her keys and purse, he locked the car and returned to his vehicle. The time read just past eight. He dialed the number of the lab, spoke with the woman in charge, explaining the circumstances. She agreed to rush the results and would call him as soon as had something for him.

He drove to the office, grabbed another cup of coffee and dropped into his desk chair.

"Gilford!" the chief bellowed.

Jake groaned. "Yep." He headed for the big office.

"Find anything last night?"

"We did. The team found a sophisticated digital player in the ceiling of Joss's bedroom. Roy's having it checked out." He looked at his boss. Apparently he wasn't the only one who hadn't slept well. Taylor looked like death warmed over. "Everything okay, Chief?"

"No! This case is taking too long. I need you on other matters."

"Unfortunately, there was an accident last night. Jocelyn Wheeler's in the hospital, unconscious. I absolutely need to follow through on this, before I take a new case."

Taylor didn't appear surprised, which made Jake wonder how much the man already knew—and if he was looking for a reason to pull him off the case.

The chief stepped closer and spoke under his breath. "When I say I need you on other matters, I expect you to comply. It's not up for discussion."

"Edward Cooper was your friend. You asked me to take care of this for you. I don't—"

"What part of *'not up for discussion'* don't you understand?" Taylor boomed. "Wrap up what you're doing. Turn in your notes to me by noon."

"Yes, sir." Jake backed out of the office. *Like hell.* He'd be out of the office in ten minutes and wouldn't come back until Taylor had calmed down. Obviously, something bigger bothered the man. Jake figured he must be in the wrong place at the wrong time.

Straightening his desk, the flashing light on the phone caught his attention. *Damned voicemail.* The only calls he wanted were from the lab or the hospital, and he'd given both of them his cell number. He knew he had to take a moment to check it, so he sat, pushed buttons, and listened.

The first three calls were of little importance. The fourth one made him sit up in his chair. "This is Sandra Kay from the post office. Someone picked up the mail in box 272, and we got a pretty clear surveillance camera shot of him. I left it at the customer service desk in an envelope with your name on it. Thanks, bye."

"Bingo!" Jake slapped the top of his desk. If he'd caught a break, there'd be a picture of Roland Watkins getting mail for Eugene Tuttle, and things would be shaping up nicely. He glanced at his watch. The post office was across town, the hospital closer and on the way. He'd stop and check on Joss first.

A nurse outside Joss's room stopped him. "One visitor at a time in the ICU."

He glanced through the window and could just make out the black arm of someone sitting in the chair next to the bed. "Who's in there?"

"She said she was the patient's mother."

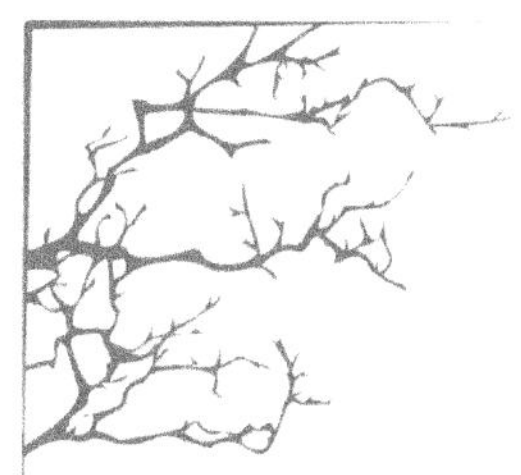

Chapter Ten

JAKE FORCED HIS JAW to remain closed, but it wasn't easy. He was shocked. Why was Joss's mother here? How had she found out about the accident? "I need to speak with her," he said decisively, wondering about the woman. Holding up his badge, he said, "Police business."

"I'll get her," the nurse agreed and motioned him away from the door.

He moved, but watched the door closely, so the woman wouldn't disappear. He highly doubted she was Joss's mother, but didn't know who in the hell she could be.

The woman followed the nurse from the room, and he approached her. Her skin appeared dark, much darker than Joss's, but that would be normal, he reminded himself. He searched her face for any resemblance. She looked nice enough, but nothing convinced him of her identity.

"You're a police officer?" she asked in a tired voice. Her eyes looked tired too.

Another person who didn't get much sleep.

"I'm Detective Jake Gilford, KCPD. I'm also a friend of Joss's. May I ask who you are?"

"Jocelyn doesn't have any friends in this place. She's only been here a short while and she's not staying. In fact, I'll probably take her home when she's released."

"You're her mother?" he asked again, because she hadn't offered.

"Yes, I'm her mother. I'm Miranda Wheeler."

"I'm sorry, Ms. Wheeler, but I need to see some identification. Joss is in the middle of a police investigation, and I firmly believe someone tried to hurt her."

"Who would want to hurt my baby?"

"That's what I'm trying to figure out. Could I see that ID, please?"

The woman stared at him with steely eyes then opened her purse and pulled out her wallet. She removed a Louisiana driver's license and handed it to him.

He studied the license. Miranda Wheeler, New Orleans. The picture looked right, it was obviously her license. Handing it back, he forced his voice to sound soft. "How did you know she was here? I planned to call you, but was waiting for some news."

"I just knew. Mothers know these things."

"I see." *What a load of bullshit.* "Guess more mothers should become detectives."

"Can I go back to my daughter, please?"

"I'd like a minute with her first."

Miranda stared at him then nodded and stepped into the waiting room. He entered Joss's room and stood at the side of her bed. She looked the same as when he had left.

"Hey, sweetheart." Jake bent and kissed her cheek. "I sure wish you'd wake up. I've got so much to tell you."

He left his face pressed to hers for a moment then straightened. "I'll be back soon. If you wake up before then, they'll call me. I love you, Joss. Remember that."

She didn't move a muscle; there was no indication that she had heard him. He hoped she had. On his way out, he passed her mother. "I may have more questions, later."

"I'll be here," she replied, before returning to Joss.

Jake watched her go then left the hospital. On the way to the post office, he thought about Miranda Wheeler. Joss hadn't spoken of her much, so he really didn't know what to expect. She seemed decent enough, but these weren't normal times, and the woman was high on his list of suspects.

Anxious to see who else made the top of his list, he hurried inside the old, brick building. Thanking the clerk behind the counter, he ripped the envelope open. He was disappointed to find there wasn't a photo of Roland Watkins inside, but instead a much younger man. A clear shot, the dark-haired man should easily be identifiable, if Jake had any idea who the hell he might be.

On a hunch, he drove to Watkins' law office. Betty was at her desk when he walked in, and he smiled.

"Well, hey, Detective." She returned the smile. "Did you have an appointment? I'm afraid Mr. Watkins isn't here."

"No, Betty, I came to see you." He held out the photo. "Do you recognize this man?"

She took it and looked at it closely. "No, I don't believe I do."

"It's not Devon Watkins?"

"Devon?" She looked again. "Not a chance."

Jake's hopes sank. "You're sure?"

"Positive. Look." She motioned him back to her employer's office. On a side table there were several framed photos. Betty picked one up. "This is Devon."

Jake studied the picture. No doubt about it, Devon Watkins was short and blonde. The man in the other photo appeared taller, with dark hair. "Thanks." He handed the picture back, and she returned it to the table.

She studied the post office photo again. "Come to think of it, this man does look vaguely familiar. Follow me." She nodded toward the door, walked out and down the hall. Another secretary sat at a desk around the corner from Betty's.

"Mary, take a look at this." She handed the picture to the middle-aged blonde woman. "Does this guy look familiar, or am I imagining things?"

"Sure, that's Nick Taylor. He works with Devon at Starlight Music, remember?"

"Of course!" She handed the photo back to Jake. "Nick Taylor, that's it. I've seen him in here a few times with Devon."

His heart pounded loudly. "Nick Taylor. I've heard that name before."

"Probably," Mary agreed. "His father's a cop. A high ranking one, I think. Maybe even chief of something."

"Chief of Detectives," he added, smiling grimly. His mind raced with possibilities—none of them good.

"Then you might know him," Mary said innocently.

He didn't answer her directly. "Thanks so much, both of you. You've been a tremendous help."

They smiled, and he left them chatting as he let himself out of the office. *Nick Taylor?* What the devil was going on? Before he could wrap his mind around this new twist, his cell phone rang. He snapped it open and barked, "Gilford."

"Jake, this is Donna from the lab. Did I catch you at a bad time?"

"No, I'm sorry," he softened his tone. "Busy day. You got something for me?"

"Oh, yeah. Would you believe dried mushrooms?"

"I'm assuming you mean the psychedelic kind, not Portabellas?"

She chuckled. "I do. They're actually called Psilocybin mushrooms. I can spell it for you." She spelled the name, and he copied it to his notepad.

"What do you know about them?"

"The side effects vary, depending on the dosage. Generally, they can cause hallucinations, mania, lethargy, depression—the usual psychedelic drug reactions. Kind of like tripping on LSD, if you remember that far back to your college days."

"Hey, I resent that. I was a good kid in college."

"So was I, Jake, but I liked to have fun."

"Okay. I'm not admitting to anything, but I had a little fun myself." Changing the subject, he continued, "So these mushrooms, a low dose over a long term—how harmful is that?"

"It can't be good. Actually, it depends on the person, the dosage, and the strength of the particular batch of mushrooms. They lose a little potency when dried, but if she ingested enough—"

"She ingested gallons of the tea, I witnessed that. Any lasting side effects, you think?"

"I wish I could tell you. Ask the docs at the hospital. They can advise you more specifically about her recovery."

"Okay, Donna, thanks."

"Oh! I forgot to mention...these mushrooms? This particular strain is indigenous to the South, if that helps at all."

"It does. Thanks again." Jake punched his phone off and shoved it back in his pocket. His breathing was rapid, nerves stretched to the limit. He couldn't shake the feeling that the more he dug, the deeper he sank into a pile of something that didn't smell good *at all*.

THE DOCTORS AT THE hospital were happy to get the name of the drug. Jake left them with Joss, plotting her new course of treatment, while he searched for her mother. He found her at a table in the cafeteria, eating a bowl of soup.

"We need to talk." He sat in a chair across from her.

"I'm having a quick bite to eat then I must get back to my daughter."

"The doctors are with her. We found out about the mushrooms. Now that they know what made her sick, they can treat her properly."

He watched her for a reaction. When she gave none, he pressed on. "Of course, you've known all along. You sat by her side quietly, wasting valuable time—time that the doctors could have spent giving her an antidote for the crap you used to poison her."

"You're wrong," she said, without much conviction. "You don't understand."

"I understand that poisoning someone is a felony, lady, whether she's your kid or not! That just makes it sicker in my book. Your daughter is going to be heartbroken when she wakes up. *If* she wakes up."

"Of course she's going to wake up! She'll be fine, and I'm taking her home." Miranda seemed in denial about the whole thing.

Jake fumed. He leaned in, hands gripping the table, and tried to control his voice so he wouldn't shout. "She almost died! Do you get that? She was whacked out on the drugs you gave her and took a walk off a roof. I held her up by a scrap of fabric. If the other officers hadn't gotten to us when they did—"

He shuddered. He hadn't let himself think about what might have happened, but he knew it was true. Joss had come very close to dying, and people close to her, and him, were responsible for it. He stared into the tearful eyes of her mother. "She almost died."

"It wasn't supposed to happen that way," she sobbed. "David promised me. I swear! The tea was lightly drugged—"

"Do you have any idea how much of that tea she drank? She started drinking it when she woke up in the morning. She drank it all day long. She had more in the middle of the night when she couldn't sleep."

Her eyes squinted. "How do you know what she did in the middle of the night?"

Jake inhaled and sat back. In his anger, he'd gone too far. Her mother didn't need to find out about them like this. *Her mother*, he scoffed. *What kind of a mother did this to her child?* Still in a state of disbelief, he couldn't imagine what Joss would say when she found out.

His cell phone rang, and he flipped it open. "Gilford."

"Detective, this is Rhonda at the ICU nurses' station. She's awake!"

"I'm on my way." He snapped his phone closed and looked at Miranda gravely. "We need to go."

After her admission, he didn't intend to let her out of his sight. They rode the elevator to the intensive care unit, and he grabbed a security guard from the waiting room. Flashing his badge, he said, "Keep this woman here. Don't let her leave."

Pointing at Miranda, he said, "Sit."

"But—my daughter!"

"I'll check on Joss. You wait here." He turned to the guard again. "I'll call for backup. Someone will be here soon. Do *not* let her leave."

"You got it," the man said and stood his ground.

Jake cast an annoyed glance at Miranda, used his phone to call for a couple of uniformed officers, then headed into Joss's room. He found her sitting up, with both the doctor and nurse examining her.

"Hey," she said to him.

He tried to sound calm and glib. "Look at you, all awake and pretty."

"I bet." She laughed, raising her arms, which were attached to tubes and needles.

"How do you feel?"

"Tired. Kind of achy. I don't remember much...like how I got here."

"What's the prognosis, Doc?" he asked the doc.

"We need to run a few more tests, but she responded immediately to the treatment. Except for the events of last night, she seems to have no loss of memory. She knew the date, the president, and a bunch of other fascinating trivia."

"What a relief!" Jake knew it wasn't appropriate in front of the doctor and a nurse, but he couldn't help himself—he slipped his arms around Joss and hugged her to his chest. "Thank God," he murmured into her hair, as she nestled against him.

"Thank you," she whispered. "I know you saved me."

He pulled back and smiled stiffly. "Let's talk about that later. Right now, we have a more serious problem."

"I dreamed my mother was here."

"*That* would be our problem."

"She kept apologizing to me, over and over. Why was she doing that, Jake?"

He couldn't lie to her. Taking a deep breath, he said, "Your tea bags were infused with hallucinogenic mushrooms, something that's common to the South. When I confronted your mother, she said the tea was only *lightly drugged.*"

"She drugged me?" Her eyes widened and filled with tears. "But why? Why would she do that?"

"That's what I'm going to find out. I'll need your help." He looked at the doctor then the nurse. "I'll need your help as well."

HE LEFT THE ICU ROOM and found two uniformed officers standing with the security guard. Miranda hadn't moved; she looked deflated and worn out. Jake planned to capitalize on those feelings, hopefully to get her to crack. "Thank you," he told the guard then held out a hand. "Cuffs?"

One officer handed over his handcuffs.

Jake guided Miranda to stand and reached for one of her hands, snapping the cuff around her wrist. "We'll leave your hands in front, as long as you cooperate."

"What are you doing?" she whimpered.

He cuffed her second wrist. "You're under arrest for the attempted murder of Jocelyn Wheeler."

"Attempted murder? No!" the woman screamed. The sound of alarms going off drowned out her sobs.

The light over the door to Joss's room flashed red. Someone yelled, "We need a crash cart in here! Stat!" Doctors and nurses rushed into the room, pushing equipment and each other out of the way.

Miranda looked frozen with fear. Jake watched her, trying to get a read on the woman. He was still mystified how a mother could poison her own child.

Muffled sounds of doctors and nurses came from Joss's room. Jake paced the floor in the hall, continuing to watch for any reaction from Miranda.

Eventually the activity stilled, and slowly the staff filtered out, grave expressions on their faces. The doctor stepped into the hall, glanced around for Jake. "Detective?"

"Yes?" He moved to the doctor, spoke with him for a moment then turned to face the other officers. "Amend the charge to murder. Jocelyn Wheeler just died."

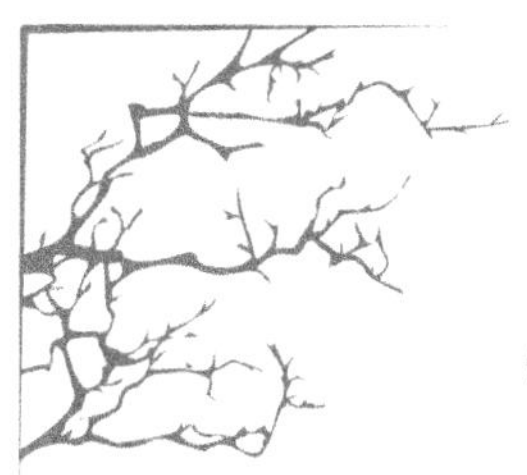

Chapter Eleven

"NO!" MIRANDA SCREAMED and fell to her knees.

Jake felt a flash of guilt, but it was necessary. Somebody wanted Joss dead. He had to figure out who.

The two cops lifted her mother into a seat. She sobbed uncontrollably as Jake watched, judging her performance.

He handed a list of names and phone numbers to the nurse. "Please phone these people, tell them what's happened and ask them to come immediately. Is there a room we can use?"

"Sure." She showed him to a private waiting room, where he left Miranda and her two bodyguards.

"Is there a computer I can use to access the Internet?"

"Yes, in the doctors' lounge. This way." She showed him to the computer.

Jake typed David Taylor's name into the police department database. He scanned the information that popped up, until he found what he was looking for. "There we go." He slapped the table next to the computer.

A doctor on the sofa glanced up.

"Sorry." He smiled sheepishly. Another thought occurred to him, and he searched the database until satisfied he was on the right track. It all seemed amazingly clear now. Completely crazy, unbelievable, but clear.

He returned to Joss's room and watched out the hall window, so he could see when people arrived. Roy was directed to the waiting room, then Roland Watkins. When David Taylor showed up, Jake knew it was time to move. His chief didn't look pleased about being summoned and he might not stick around long.

"Let's go." He settled Joss in a wheelchair, attached her IV bags to a transportable pole which he rolled along next to her. He parked her in an adjacent waiting room and stepped inside the one where everyone else was gathered.

"What's going on here, Gilford?" Taylor asked immediately.

He ignored his chief and looked at Roy. "Thanks for coming. You have a set of cuffs, I hope? We'll need them."

"I do." Roy folded his arms across his chest. "I'm real sorry to hear about Joss. What's up?"

Jake looked at the nervous faces of Roland Watkins and Miranda Wheeler. "I guess the younger Watkins and Taylor boys aren't going to make an appearance." He turned to one of the uniformed officers. "Make a call, have someone pick them up for questioning."

"What the devil are you talking about?" Taylor shouted. "I'm sure you're upset that the girl died, but—"

"You know," Jake interrupted. "I am upset. But not about Joss. She's going to be fine." He yanked open the door connecting the two waiting rooms and wheeled her in.

"Jocelyn!" her mother cried.

Taylor, obviously shocked, bellowed, "She's alive!"

"Sorry about the deception, but somebody in this room wanted her dead. Now, we get to watch and see who's the most disappointed."

"None of them look very happy," Joss muttered.

"I'm happy!" Roy flashed a big grin.

Jake smiled at him then returned his attention to the group. "Okay, people, here's what we know, so far. It's a long, messy story, so I'll be as succinct as possible. Edward Cooper died, leaving his large estate to a daughter he never knew, apparently the result of a fling some twenty-five years ago. Joss came here to settle the estate and has had nothing but problems since she arrived. Someone obviously tried to scare her out of the mansion—a delightful skeleton in the attic, thunderously loud noises every night and Lord knows what else was there that we didn't uncover.

"The noises we traced to a sophisticated piece of digital equipment, planted in the ceiling of her room. Thanks to Chief Roy Nelson of the Surveillance Bureau, for uncovering that." He nodded to Roy, who smiled and waved at the others.

Jake paced the floor as he gathered his thoughts. "When I got a copy of Cooper's will, I discovered if anything happened to Joss, the sizeable estate—we're talking millions—would go to a charity called *Save Our Wildlife*. This surprised me, until I looked into the organization. There are three officers listed, Ross Whitcomb, William Rust, and Eugene Tuttle. I found quite a lot about Whitcomb and Rust on the Internet, the most recent and most interesting being their obituaries. They're both dead."

Joss looked up at him, her mouth agape.

He nodded at her and continued. "There is nothing on the Internet about Eugene Tuttle. Coincidentally, though, a man by the name of Eugene Tuttle rented an office on the same floor as the Watkins law practice."

Jake paused and looked at Roland Watkins. "You said you didn't know him, Watkins."

"I don't," the lawyer insisted.

"Tuttle, the invisible man." Jake smiled to himself. "Well, Mr. Tuttle's mail is forwarded to a post office box. This is a photo of the man who got the mail from that box yesterday." He held up the picture, and everyone squinted to see it. "Here, Chief." Jake handed it to his boss. "Recognize him?"

The chief merely glared at the photo.

"It's his son," Jake told the others. "Nick Taylor, a man who—again, coincidentally—works at Starlight Music with Devon Watkins, Roland's son." He nodded toward the lawyer.

"It's a perfectly legitimate business," Taylor said. "I told you, I knew Watkins."

"I'm sure the business is legit," Jake agreed. "I'm sure they also use sophisticated digital recording equipment, like the player found in Joss's ceiling."

"Oh!" Joss murmured, putting it all together.

"You can't prove a thing," Watkins muttered.

"That's where you're wrong, Watkins. You see, I fancy myself a pretty good detective. I'm no Sam Spade, of course, but I didn't have to be. The evidence in this case just fell into my lap. David Taylor and Edward Cooper were old friends. In fact, I saw in the chief's bio, which I read online today, that he used to work as an insurance investigator before he joined the department. That was about twenty-five years ago." He looked at his boss. "You worked with Cooper, didn't you?"

"I told you we were old friends," Taylor muttered through gritted teeth.

"Yes, and Miranda told me so much more than that. She admitted to drugging Joss's teabags with Psilocybin mushrooms, which made her daughter gravely ill, in fact, almost caused her death. Miranda told me, *'David said it would be okay.'* So the only thing left to wonder is why. Why bother with the scare tactics at the house? You obviously didn't want Joss to inherit the money. The only way to keep that from happening was to kill her. There would have been easier ways to accomplish that, so either we're looking at a very stupid bunch of crooks—"

"No one wanted to kill her!" Miranda cried, rising to her feet. "We just wanted to frighten her a little. The Voodoo Priestess who sold me the mushrooms in New Orleans assured me they were safe in low doses."

"Shut up," Taylor snarled.

"A Voodoo Priestess? This just gets better and better." Jake shook his head.

Joss looked at her. "You know how much tea I drink. You could've killed me!"

"I wanted you to come home," her mother sobbed, dropping to her knees. She inched her way to the front of Joss's wheelchair, crying and talking at the same time. "David promised me this would work. We just wanted to scare you out of the house, so you'd come home to me of your own free will. I couldn't have you stay here."

"Because she might discover the truth?" Jake asked. He inhaled, plastered on his poker face, and bluffed to see what would happen. "I saw Edward Cooper's medical file. He was sterile. He couldn't be Joss's father."

Joss stared up at him, and Jake prayed he'd deduced correctly. Miranda soon confirmed it. "David said it would be better this way. Edward had much more money. The weekend they came through town on business was a blur to him. He spent the whole time passed out, drunk. He never knew what happened."

"You mean, he never knew if you slept together or not," Jake said. "But while Edward was passed out, you had sex with David."

"Don't say another word," Taylor commanded.

"It doesn't matter, Miranda," Jake told her. "We know the truth now. You lied about the identity of Joss's father, to her and to Cooper. You were thrilled when he left his estate to her. What you didn't know, is that Taylor and Watkins had no intention of letting her inherit the estate. They set up a phony charity and sat back while you poisoned your daughter to death. You'd take the fall, they'd be clear to inherit the estate."

"You're crazy," Taylor muttered, "and you can't prove a thing."

Jake's cell phone rang. He checked the screen, snapped it open. "Gilford. Yeah, go ahead." He listened for a minute then said, "Okay, thanks." He closed the phone and smiled like the Cheshire Cat. "Devon Watkins just confessed that he and Nick Taylor were planting things in the mansion, setting up the digital player to go off every night and, most interestingly, putting more drugs in Joss's teabags. She was getting double doses."

"Oh no!" Joss looked down at her mother sniveled at her feet.

Jake turned to Roy. "I'd like you to place Mr. Watkins, here, under arrest, along with Joss's mother and father. Attempted murder is the first complaint. That ought to hold them while we figure out the rest of the charges."

"I'll have your badge for this!" Taylor exploded, his face beet red.

"No, Sir, I believe I'll have yours." Jake stared at him defiantly.

Taylor's eyes widened. He let loose with a string of expletives.

Roy stepped forward. "My, my, my. In front of your daughter and her mama. You should be ashamed of yourself."

Taylor glared, started to speak again then appeared to notice Miranda and Joss watching him. The fight left him, and he dropped back into his chair.

"I'll take care of this one," Roy told the uniformed men. "You get Watkins and the elder Ms. Wheeler, please."

"Joss, no!" Her mother clung to her legs. "Baby, don't let them do this! You know I never meant to harm you!"

"You need to go now, Miranda," Jake pried her off Joss. "Your daughter needs her rest. She's been very sick, you know. She almost died."

The woman stopped struggling and allowed the officer to lead her away. Jake and Joss watched as the three were led off.

"I need to lie down," she admitted. "I feel horrible."

"I'm not sure lying down's going to make that feeling go away, but we'll give it a try." He wheeled her back to her room.

"I can't think about this yet, Jake. I want to sleep, mull it over in my mind. I might have some questions for you."

"I'm not going anywhere," he whispered and placed a kiss on her cheek.

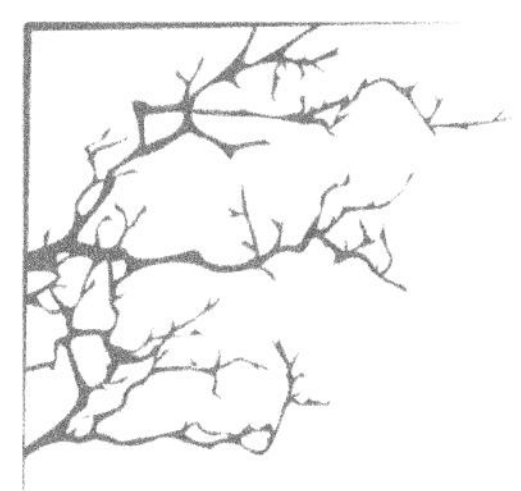

Epilogue

ONE WEEK LATER, JOSS was released from the hospital. Jake picked her up, prepared to take her to his house, but first she had a request.

"Why did you want to come here?" He parked in front of the mansion.

"I need to see it, one more time."

They walked, hand in hand, to the front door. Jake unlocked it and faced her.

She smiled at him. "This is where we met, remember?"

"Of course I remember. It seems like yesterday and a lifetime ago."

"To me, too." She stepped inside and looked around. "I never felt a connection to this house. Even going through my father's personal things, I never felt anything."

"He wasn't your father."

"I don't have a father." She sighed and shook her head. "It still doesn't seem real. I'll never claim that man who's sitting in jail for trying to kill me."

"He's going to be there for a good, long time. He and Watkins are both looking at ten to twenty-five years. Even if the judge is lenient and gives them the minimum sentence, ten years is a long time."

She turned to him and smiled, slipping her arms around his waist. "Where will we be in ten years?"

He lovingly pulled her body against his. "Ten years? Probably sitting in the bleachers at a Little League game, watching our son."

"Or our daughter."

"Hell, yeah! Our daughter can play if she wants to. She's going to be strong and beautiful, like her mama. She can be anything she wants."

Joss buried her face in his chest and sobbed. "Mothers," she whispered. "I still can't decide what to do about mine."

He rubbed her back gently. "You know how I feel. She made a mistake, but she never intended to kill you. Taylor and Watkins dreamed up that plan. Your mother was used."

"Seems she liked being used," Joss muttered. "All those years, I thought she was a waitress who fell for the wrong man. Instead, she was a hooker! Until she got lucky—getting pregnant with me and convincing Cooper to pay her off."

"Don't judge too harshly. She made a good life for you and became a nurse with the money he gave her."

"I can't forgive her for what she's done, but I can't stand to think of her in prison."

"Maybe she could benefit from probation and counseling."

"She'd have to agree to stay away. I don't want her anywhere near us."

"That might make her miserable, but I'm sure she'd do it to avoid prison. She insists she loves you, Joss."

"I know." She sighed. "Maybe someday it won't hurt so much. Maybe then, I'll let her back into my life. Only if we're sure she's changed and not a danger to our children."

"Our children," Jake mused. "I love the sound of that." He kissed the top of her head then pulled away. "So, what are we doing here?"

"I wanted to prove to myself that this house won't haunt me, before I sell it. Strange, it doesn't look scary anymore, Jake. It just looks sad."

"Sad and lonely. Like it could use some children running around to lighten the mood."

They looked at each other, smiles spreading across their faces. "You think?" she asked.

"It's your call. You've got some bad memories here. I wouldn't want to start our new life with that hanging over us."

She glanced around. "It's a lovely house. It actually feels right. Get rid of the animals, of course. Think how wonderful this place could be. Soft blue mini-blinds instead of heavy drapes, all new furniture."

"I agree. It has the potential to be a beautiful home. There'll be lots of work, and it'll be pretty expensive."

She grinned. "Good thing I'm loaded, with nothing but time on my hands. I think old Edward would like to see his house turned into a loving, family home, don't you?"

"I definitely do. I'm sure he'd be quite pleased."

She looked thoughtful. "With some effort, the rose garden out back might be the perfect place for a spring wedding."

"Get all this done by spring?" He raised his eyebrows. "My back hurts just thinking about it."

Taking his hand, she pulled him up the stairs. "You putting off our wedding?"

"Hardly! I just didn't know it hinged on doing a bunch of hard labor first."

"You're such a *guy*," she teased.

He whined, playing along. "Why are we going up here?"

"To see what needs to be done in the bedroom."

"I can think of one thing."

She glanced back at him, batting her eyelashes. "Only one? Where's your imagination, Detective?"

Jake chuckled. "Listen! Hear that?"

"What?" She paused.

"The quiet. Beautiful, blissful quiet." He pushed her up the stairs playfully.

Joss squealed, and they bounded up the steps together.

<u>Also by Jamie Hill</u>
Witness Security Series
Pieces of the Past 1
Time to Kill
Cover of Darkness
And coming soon: Darkest Before Dawn

Secrets and Lies

A Cop in the Family Series
Family Secrets
Family Ties
Family Honor
The Blame Game Series
Blame it on the Stars
Blame it on the Moon
Blame in on the Sun
Blame it on the Rain

Don't miss out!

Visit the website below and you can sign up to receive emails whenever Jamie Hill publishes a new book. There's no charge and no obligation.

https://books2read.com/r/B-A-GXCU-LZPZB

BOOKS 2 READ

Connecting independent readers to independent writers.

Did you love *On the Edge*? Then you should read *Secrets and Lies*[1] by Jamie Hill!

Natalie Jameson has a handsome husband, three wonderful children, and one very big secret. She's managed to keep it under wraps for over twenty years, but recent events lead her to decide she has no choice but to reveal the terrible truth. Alex Jameson has had one goal in life since the minute he met Natalie on their college campus. *Do whatever it takes to make this woman happy.* When circumstances threaten to unravel the web of secrets and lies they've built around themselves, will their love be strong enough to survive?

"Author Jamie Hill has a knack for pulling a reader deeper and deeper into her stories as they try to figure out where she is leading them." ~ Tammy, Fallen Angel Reviews

---

1. https://books2read.com/u/4ELZRe

2. https://books2read.com/u/4ELZRe

Read more at https://books2read.com/ap/xqlaam/Jamie-Hill.

About the Author

Jamie Hill filled up one notebook after another, writing as a young adult. She picked up the craft again years later, tapping on the computer late at night after putting her children to bed. First published in 2005, she's written numerous novels and short stories.

Jamie lives in the Midwest where she enjoys spending time with her family, streaming true crime shows, crocheting, and snuggling warm, cuddly puppies.

Read more at https://books2read.com/ap/xqlaam/Jamie-Hill.